...peace, some hooch, some cake—all Mitch wants is to walk down the aisle with Sam Keller, have a party, and live happily ever after. But every day of wedding planning brings a new set of handicaps, legal, logistical, and emotional…until he brings in his best friend, Randy Jansen.

Randy loves being the third point in Sam and Mitch's kinky triangle, and nothing would give him more pleasure than to thumb his nose at small-town snobbery and give Iowa the most fantastic gay wedding it's ever seen. But as his plan comes together and his friends prepare to sail off into the sunset, Randy begins to consider the unthinkable: that maybe, just maybe, he wishes he could have a little hooch and cake of his own.

This book is a work of fiction. The names, characters, places, and incidents are products of the writer's imagination or have been used fictitiously and are not to be construed as real. Any resemblance to persons, living or dead, actual events, locale, or organizations is entirely coincidental.

Heidi Cullinan, POB 425, Ames, Iowa 50010

Copyright © 2017 by Heidi Cullinan
Print ISBN: 978-1-945116-26-1
Edited by Sasha Knight
Cover by Kanaxa
Proofing by Lillie's Literary Services
Formatting by BB eBooks

All Rights Are Reserved. No part of this book may be used or reproduced in any manner whatsoever without written permission, except in the case of brief quotations embodied in critical articles and reviews.

First publication 2017
www.heidicullinan.com

HOOCH AND CAKE

HEIDI CULLINAN

for the lighthouses

ACKNOWLEDGMENTS

Thanks to Ann, who gave me the idea for the title.

Thank you to Leigh and Dan for light-speed beta work. Love you both to bits and pieces.

Thanks, again, to Adam at Wheatsfield Cooperative for not just giving *Special Delivery* its germ but for being so cool about the whole thing. And for Andrew for teaching me how to spell tszuj. Which I didn't end up using in this novella, but it's certainly on my bucket list now.

Thanks as always to my patrons, especially Rosie M., Pamela Bartual, Kaija Kovanen, Marie, Sarah Plunkett, Erin Sharpe, and Sarah M.

AUTHOR'S NOTES

This novella takes place after *Special Delivery* but before *Double Blind*. Because of the timeline when the first and second books were originally written, the Defense of Marriage Act is still in place for this story. This story probably makes the most sense after reading book one, but if you want to read this out of order, nobody's going to show up at your door and arrest you. You'll have the ending spoiled for *Special Delivery*, except it's a romance, so you kind of knew they were going to get together anyway.

If you read this short and decide you'd like to try the other books in the series, check out www.heidicullinan.com or look for more details in the back of this book.

CHAPTER ONE

Mitch Tedsoe didn't regret proposing to Sam Keller, since there wasn't anything more he wanted in the world than to spend the rest of his life with the man he loved. But it turned out getting to that happily ever after wasn't quite as simple as he'd thought it would be.

Some of it was easy. Mitch knew they'd live in Middleton, Iowa, until Sam finished school, and after that they'd wander nomadically around the country in Old Blue, Sam taking short-term positions in an area where Mitch could get regular trucking gigs. When they got married, they'd be hyphenating their names. Mitch had been ready to shift over to Keller, because God knew he didn't need any ties to his blood family, but Sam had pointed out *Tedsoe Trucking* not only had a rep but a nice ring to it, so they compromised with the hyphen.

But first they had to actually have the ceremony. Mitch had no designs on how that happened, so when Sam's best friend, Emma, got engaged too, and they began to plot and scheme for romantic ceremonies together, Mitch let Sam and his friend set everything up.

He had to get a best man, they told him, so he called Randy Jansen.

"I wondered when you were going to ask." Randy sounded almost annoyed. "I'd started worrying you'd made some *other* best friend off in your Midwestern paradise."

"Well, I always figured you'd be there, Skeet. I just didn't know if Sam would want something simple or elaborate."

Randy snorted. "Are you kidding me? Peaches was always going to be about the full experience, but not in a fancy way, either. So a bit of both, really." He sighed happily, and Mitch could imagine him settling in on his couch. "What do you want me to work on first? The ceremony or the reception?"

"Wait—what?"

"Come on. You can't tell me *you* want to plan a party."

"Well, no, but I think Sam does."

Mitch wasn't sure how Randy could make an eye roll audible, but he managed it. "Fine. When you get stuck, call me."

"*Hey.* I'm not going to get stuck. Sam's got this. Planning it with his friend Emma. She's getting married too."

Another snort. "*Oh, excellent.* You'll be calling me inside of a month."

Now Mitch was pissed. "No, we won't. If Sam has trouble, I'll help him."

"You'll call me before Christmas. I'll keep my schedule clear."

The fuck Mitch was calling him with anything but a date and a place and instructions for what to wear. He could do this. Or rather, he could help Sam do this. How hard could it be?

The answer, he discovered, was pretty fucking hard.

The worst part was that it wasn't hard because weddings were a bitch—or, at least not *only* that. Mitch and Sam had an extra handicap, one with an ugly underbelly. It started when they tried to find a place for the ceremony. Sam wasn't a churchgoer, which relieved the hell out of Mitch, but ruling out houses of worship didn't leave a lot of attractive prospects in Middleton. Mitch assumed they'd get married in some rented hall then transform it into a dance floor and party. Problem was, there were two hotels in Middleton, both middle-grade chains that had little personality and no empathy for equality. While the managers didn't refuse to let them book anything, they put such a damper on Sam's enthusiasm that Mitch took over the search for somewhere to get married.

Except their other options were the American Legion Hall, the Knights of Columbus Hall, and the pavilion at the city park. The first two options came with even more icy glances and cutting remarks, and the last one just seemed really fucking pathetic. Fine for the ceremony, but what about afterward?

Mitch couldn't help noticing Emma and Steve had no trouble at all with their plans. They were getting married at the Catholic Church in September and having a reception at some fancy hotel in Ames. Mitch had immediately called up the events planner there, thinking the college town had to be more open-minded than Middleton. It was, and they were thrilled to host another same-sex couple. They'd had twenty already that year.

They also had few open dates and wanted more for a deposit than Mitch had left in the bank.

What had been a decent-sized savings account when his rent wasn't more than a post office box in Denver depleted quickly when he ponied up his and Sam's half of the apartment, and when Emma moved out to live with *her* fiancé, Mitch forked over the full amount. Sam covered food and utilities, but with school, that was all he could manage. Delia and Norm had given him a loan, but paying the monthly payments was a stress for him. His uncle was more easygoing, but his aunt tended to lecture him if he didn't offer a particular amount, so as much as possible Mitch made sure the only thing Sam had to pay for around the house was the loan.

Better for Sam. Living hell on Mitch's wallet. Covering the bills meant being on the road a lot more, which was part of why it took Mitch so long to figure out there was trouble.

Emma's parents were paying for her ceremony. Steve's were buying the booze and giving them three grand for a down payment on a house in town.

Randy called Mitch. Often. "How's the planning?" he'd always ask.

"Fine," Mitch would bite off, and change the subject.

Except it wasn't fine. Every day that passed illustrated how different Emma's experience was than Sam's. Emma went dress shopping with her mother and worried over the cut of bridesmaid gowns. Sam looked at a few tuxedos, but since they had nowhere to wear them and no date locked down, that was as far as it went. Emma planned for a honeymoon in Hawaii. Sam, still stuck on square one, got excited when he found out a local winery had a reception area—until he found out the rental price was three grand. Before catering.

Eventually Sam suggested they give up and go to the courthouse.

Mitch balked. "But that's not what you

wanted."

Sam shrugged. "We can't find anywhere we can afford or that won't make us feel unwelcome, and really, outside of Emma and Randy and a few friends from the community college, who's going to come?"

The comment about nobody coming burned because it was true. Mitch's contribution to the guest list was Randy. His mom wouldn't come up from Houston, not unless he offered her money. If Cooper Tedsoe showed up, Mitch would step on his neck. Mitch had renewed a few acquaintances the last couple times they'd been through Vegas, but nobody who would haul ass all the way to Iowa for a wedding. Sam's aunt and uncle had made it clear they didn't want to come, and they were the only family he had. Sam didn't hang out with many people from school outside of Emma, and Mitch didn't socialize much in town.

They didn't need a wedding hall. They needed a wedding *hallway*.

"No," Mitch told Sam. "We're going to have a real wedding. Hooch and cake and the whole bit."

Sam laughed. "Hooch and cake?"

"Yes. Hooch and cake and dancing and friends looking on while we go down the aisle. It's going to happen. I'm going to *make* it work."

But he couldn't. Every hour of every run, Mitch noodled over the wedding, trying to find the way to make it small and special too. He could think of a million things to do at places they'd visited on their travels, but it had to be in *Iowa*, and not just because Sam was sentimental. Their marriage had to occur in one of the handful of places where it would be legal.

As the year wore on, Emma pored over bridal catalogs and went to wedding fairs and looked at fabric samples with stars in her eyes, and Sam got quieter and quieter, until he didn't bring up getting married in any way, ever, at all.

In November Mitch gave up. Randy answered on the third ring, and from the noise in the background, Mitch could hear a poker game going on.

"I just want you to note, Old Man," Randy began blithely, "that even though you're chafing at having to grovel, I left a table full of fish to take your call. It's not losing to ask me for help. It's wisely using all your assets."

Mitch grunted and slumped deeper into the couch.

When Randy spoke again, his voice was silky. "It's not losing. But I am going to be bitch enough to make you *ask*."

Mitch rolled his eyes at the ceiling then did his best to make his tone sound contrite. "Skeet, I need you to help me plan my wedding."

"Of course. I'll book a flight right now."

Mitch softened. "Thanks."

"Anytime, Old Man. Any fucking time."

The Friday before Thanksgiving, Mitch and Sam met him at the baggage claim of the Omaha airport, where Skeet sauntered toward them, rubbing his bare arms against the Midwest November chill and grinning like the maniacal bastard he was.

"Good afternoon, ladies." He gripped Mitch in a tight hug, pressing a kiss on his cheek before taking Sam into his arms and spinning him around until Sam laughed and demanded to be put down. Randy openly palmed Sam's ass as he leered at Mitch. "What sort of trouble have we been getting up to since I last saw you?"

Sam told Randy about school, and Mitch offered up some stories from a few runs to Wisconsin, but not a word was said by anyone about the wedding. Mitch worried Randy would bring it up and spoil the mood, but he didn't so much as hint at the reason he'd been called away from Vegas.

He did, however, begin pawing at Sam the hot second they got to the car.

Technically Randy had begun playing around the second he'd met them inside the airport, touching Sam every chance he got, but as soon as they were at the vehicle, he got serious. For one, he didn't let Sam sit up front with Mitch, but rather he drew Mitch's fiancé into the back seat with him, hauling Sam into his lap and whispering darkly into his ear as Sam made weak protestations and squirmed against his touch. Before Mitch got out of the parking lot, wicked murmurs and pleading gasps made him adjust his rearview mirror so he could see Randy's hand disappear into Sam's unzipped jeans.

"I don't want to be seen by the parking lot attendant." Sam said this, but he also arched his back and spread his legs wider to give Randy access to his crotch.

Mitch adjusted the mirror again to get a better angle of that action and slowed down so he could drive and watch without risking an accident.

"Take off your coat and use it to cover yourself." When Sam only mewled, Randy sucked on Sam's ear and shrugged out of his own jacket.

Sam whined when Randy let go of him to pull his arm out and drape the garment over him.

Who knew what the parking attendant thought, and hell if Mitch gave a damn. All he knew was that by the time they hit the first stoplight outside of the airport area, Sam was begging, promising to blow Randy all the way home if he'd let Sam come.

"You'll do that anyway, sweet little slut." Randy bit Sam's ear, making him squeal.

"Why don't you get started on that blowjob right now, though?"

Mitch grinned and fumbled for his cigarettes, keeping one eye on the mirror as Randy maneuvered Sam on the seat until his mouth was on Randy's cock, and Randy's hand was down the back of his pants. Mouth full of dick, Sam whimpered, and Mitch let pleasure burn through him like the smolder of his tobacco.

Sunshine, love, there's no way he's gonna let you come until Middleton. A two-hour drive away.

Mitch wished it were four hours, honestly. This show was going to be *great*.

"That's it, baby." Randy put a hand on the back of Sam's head and guided the blowjob with dark pleasure. "All the way to the back of your throat." His fingers slipped deeper, and Sam let out a high-pitched whine. Randy smiled. "That's right. Let the old man hear you sucking my cock. Let him hear how hot you are for some guy you picked up at the airport who sticks a finger in your ass." He guided the blowjob a few minutes more then frowned at Sam's hair. "Peaches, what the fuck did you do to your mop?"

Mitch grunted around his Winston. "Highlights. Emma did it to him." He let the image of Sam's swollen mouth moving up and down Randy's dick fill his head before he had to pay attention to an on-ramp to the interstate. "Thinks he wants to be blond."

Randy snorted and tightened his grip on Sam's hair. "I'll put white in your hair, kid. Enough cum shampoos and you ought to go blond. We can start right now."

Sam made desperate noises around his mouthful, and Mitch met Randy's gaze in the mirror. "Too far. He won't want anyone in Middleton to see. And don't even try to get him into a public display in the backseat. Car's too low. You're lucky you're getting what you are now."

"Oh, yes. We're in the land of family values." Randy rolled his eyes and palmed Sam's ass, sliding his waistband down. "On your face, then, hon. When I give you a slap, pull up and open your mouth."

It was a good show—hot as fuck, though Mitch didn't miss how quick it went, Randy's deference to Sam's concern about passersby.

As promised, Randy came all over Sam's face, wiping it up with the bandana Mitch passed him from the front seat. Because *this*, Randy fucking Sam all the way back to town, Mitch had completely foreseen.

Randy kept Sam on a hair trigger, with fingers in his ass and pinches on his nipples as he whispered about all the things he was going to do to Sam. Mitch smiled and got another cigarette as Sam got horny enough to show Randy the XTube vid he wanted to recreate.

"Look at the way he pounds him." Sam held his phone with trembling hands—half because the video was damn hot, half because he was sitting on three of Randy's fingers. "The guy just holds him down and hammers him. The guy he's doing is so desperate—he's got to be going so deep and so hard, but he's taking it." Sam shivered, the expression on his face wistful. "I want that."

Mitch tapped his cigarette out the window and caught Randy's gaze in the rearview mirror. "I've tried to give it to him, but my hips don't roll the way they need to for what Sunshine's after. Figured you could manage it, though."

"Oh, I think I could, yes." Randy's voice was silk, and he made Sam gasp, fucking his fingers in and out of Sam's ass. "And you want Mitch watching that happen to you, don't you, Peaches?"

Sam's voice was strained. "Yes. I do want that. *Please.*"

"Then I guess I'll have to give it to you." There was a sharp slap of a hand against flesh, and Sam startled. "Going to give you something right now, honey. Shimmy forward between the front seats as best you can and stick your ass in the air and spread your knees."

Mitch saw Sam's flush of eagerness in the rearview mirror, but also his wariness. "What if people see—?"

"I'm putting the coat over your ass. No worries." Randy pinched Sam's ass. "Go on."

Sam crawled forward—and then Mitch wasn't watching Sam in the mirror anymore. He had only to glance to the side, because Sam was right beside him, flushed and breathing hard, holding himself up on his forearms as Randy maneuvered the rest of him behind.

He gave Mitch a shy smile. "Hi."

Mitch winked and reached over to tweak his nose. "Howdy. What's up, Sunshine?"

"Not sure yet. I—*Oh*." Sam's cheeks colored and his mouth fell open, his pupils dilating.

Mitch combed fingers through Sam's hair, petting him then settling in as a gentle anchor. "Tell me what he's doing to you, baby."

Sam's voice was shaky, occasionally breaking. "He's sucking the inside of my—*oh*—thigh, but he has…two fingers in me, and…" He stopped to grip the armrest. "He's tugging on my balls."

Mitch growled in approval and tightened his grip on Sam's hair. "He fucking you with those fingers?"

"Not…not yet. Just spreading and turning—*oh. Ah!*" Sam shut his eyes as his body was thrust forward. "N-now he is."

Mitch checked the mirror and saw Randy positioned behind Sam, arm working hard beneath his coat, which was draped over Sam's backside. Mitch nearly purred. "He using lube on you? Getting you good and wet?"

"L-lots of—*oh God*—lube. *Jesus.*" Sam gasped, his breath punctuated by the thrusts coming at his body. "So wet."

"He got more fingers in you now?"

"Yes. Three, I think."

"Gonna go for four once you get slick enough. Let you feel my knuckles in there." Randy's voice was sleek as sin. "Still working his balls, though. He likes that, don't you, Peaches?"

Sam nodded. Mitch dared a glance at him, heart skipping a beat as he saw the telltale glaze on his lover's face. Sam was going under. Hard.

Full of love, Mitch massaged the top of Sam's head. "Answer him, baby. Tell Skeet you like it when he works your balls."

Sam answered dutifully, as if from somewhere far away. "I like it when you play with my balls, Randy."

"You're getting all worked open. You're a good little slut, Sam. You like being Randy's slut, honey?"

Sam's lips parted on a soft sigh as Randy

started thrusting once more. The way Sam's body shuddered told Mitch he'd added that last finger. "I love being his slut. For you."

Mitch cast his eyes to the road again, but his heart was beside him, wrapped up in Sam getting finger fucked between the seats. He let his fingers trail down Sam's cheek, over Sam's mouth.

Sam kissed the digits, then sucked them into his mouth and whimpered around them as Randy continued his torture.

Once they entered Middleton, Sam extricated himself from Randy and buttoned himself up, trying to play it cool, even though he was shaking and clearly anything but collected. Mitch parked in their alley parking space, and as he carried Randy's suitcase up the stairs, he watched Sam squirm away from Skeet all the way into the apartment, whispering hotly about the neighbors.

They're going to explode the second they get in the door. Mitch grinned and adjusted the chub in his jeans.

Explode they did—as soon as they were inside, Randy pushed Sam face-first into the hall wall, where Sam swore, then moaned as

Randy stripped Sam's jeans to his ankles and went to work on his ass, sucking at his flesh. Mitch shut the door, locked it, and pulled up a chair to watch.

Nobody gave a show like those two, and nobody loved a front-row seat more than Mitch. The sex was hot, yes—he'd always loved playing voyeur. But with Sam and Randy, it was something special. It was the way Mitch could see, because he knew them both so well, how they let go with one another. In the year since Mitch had moved in with Sam, they'd been together three times, twice in Vegas, once on an un-fucking-forgettable trip to Florida. Every time Mitch could see how much Randy both loved and feared Sam. How much he loved that he could be himself, asshole and all, with Sam—and how much he worried any second now Sam would cut him off. That fear came out in the way he dominated Sam, a kind of desperate terror Mitch wasn't sure Sam consciously realized and yet still responded to.

It had been three months since their last hookup with each other, and they were pretty intense.

Randy ate Sam out for a good ten minutes, spreading Sam naked against the wall and licking his hole lazily while Sam pleaded at him to fuck him, sobbing when Randy only spread the opening with his hands and stuck his tongue inside.

"*Please*, Randy." Sam's whole body shook now. "Please let me come."

"Blow me first," Randy ordered, pulling away from Sam's ass and rising, leaning against the wall lazily.

Sam clambered to undo Randy's jeans and fumbled for his dick like he was a kid unwrapping a long-sought Christmas present. When he finally freed it, he cried out, then fell onto it with a grunt, sucking and moving fast—but he also cast his gaze up to Randy, because that was what Randy had trained him to do.

"Good boy." Randy watched him idly, resting a hand on Sam's hair, occasionally holding his head in place to force the cock deeper, longer into his throat. "You look good with a cock in your throat. A proper slut. Maybe later tonight I'll make you kneel in front of me, and then I'll fuck your mouth with a fat dildo for an hour. Make your mouth good and swollen, baby. As swollen as your ass is. You can feel that, can't you? Your poor ass, stuffed full of fingers for an hour. Now it's going to be pounded by dick. And you want it, don't you, Peaches? You want me to make your ass even more swollen, baby?"

Sam groaned around Randy's cock, sucking it harder, taking it to the root.

Now Randy trembled, but he laughed too, pushing Sam away. "You can't make me come yet, sweet thing. I'm coming in that ass of yours." He bent and slapped it. "Hands and knees, facing your man. Let him see your show while you get fucked."

Mitch didn't smile as Sam arranged himself, arms and legs shuddering with want. Mitch was too focused on the scene, too turned on by the knowledge Sam was seriously under Randy at the moment, so far gone he'd do about anything Randy told him to do. Mitch was also aware, however, that Sam was hyper-fixated on *him*, that though he was following Randy's commands, it was Mitch he watched, Mitch he stared at glassy-eyed as Randy pushed into him and began to fuck. He never looked away, closing his eyes only as he orgasmed, but he met Mitch's gaze again as Randy finished inside him, and as Randy pulled out to dispose of the condom, it was Mitch Sam leaned on, shaking and soft, still staring up at his face.

Not once had Mitch asked for that devotion. Not one time had Sam ever failed to give it to him.

Once Sam was less sensitized and could take another pounding, Mitch took his turn at his lover's ass, a perfunctory fucking, except he had Sam face Randy this time. That quickly degenerated, since Randy didn't like watching, he liked doing, and so soon Sam had Randy's cock in his mouth while he had Mitch's in his ass. Once everyone was sated and cleaned up, all fell into the bed in a tangle.

Sam, who'd finished a huge exam that morning, passed out in a wink. Mitch dozed for a minute, but when he woke and heard Randy in the kitchen, he shut the door to the bedroom so he could have a heart-to-heart with his oldest friend.

Randy didn't turn around as Mitch came

in, opening and shutting cupboards. "All right, wise guy. Where are the coffee filters?"

"Canister beside the fridge. The one that says *sugar*."

Randy snorted and opened it. "Guess that answers my question about whether or not I have to go to the store to make my apple pie for Thursday."

"We have sugar. It's in a bag on the round-and-round thing in the corner." When Randy gave him a murderous look, Mitch sideways smiled and took a seat at the breakfast bar. "You can rearrange. Just let Sam know what you've changed. It's been madness here since Emma moved out. He's always at school, and I'm always on the road. Don't say anything about the apartment. He cleaned like crazy, or tried to, but I made him stop last night to study."

As Mitch expected, this softened Randy, and he glanced worriedly at the closed bedroom door. "Tell me about this wedding planning. Give me every detail about what's gone wrong and why."

Mitch explained about the money, the venue, and the guest list as Randy started a pot of coffee brewing. "It doesn't help that his best friend is also planning a wedding and having exactly the opposite experience. Mom all involved, three-hundred-person guest list they're trying to whittle down to two-fifty, nobody looking down their nose when they book a place."

"You do know you can make a fuss if people refuse you service, right?"

"Yeah—but they're not saying no. If they did, it'd be better. I'd send a note to one of those gay blogs, and the whole world would be up in arms in ten minutes. They don't say no. They say *absolutely* but with their mouths in a pucker. Let me tell you, that's ten times worse."

Randy grimaced as he poured two cups of coffee, passing the first to Mitch. "I wish you could just come to Vegas. I could plan a wedding in ten minutes that would make you fifty friends for life, and you'd never wish you had anything different." He took a sip of his coffee and stared hard at the far wall as he tapped his fingers absently on the mug. Eventually he sighed and put the mug down. "One crisis at a time. Am I right in assuming there's no plan yet for Thanksgiving dinner?"

"That would be a correct assumption. Sam's got school through Wednesday, and his days are long with a lot of homework in the evenings, plus hours at the pharmacy. I gotta head out Sunday afternoon for a run to Dallas, and I'm going to try to get another gig from there if I can. I'll be back by Wednesday night for sure."

"Jesus Christ. Is this how you two've been living?"

Mitch shrugged. "Not much else to do. Rent's a bitch, and so's his aunt. He graduates at the end of next summer, but that means he's got to work like hell until then, both at school and at the pharmacy. And so do I."

"You guys are pieces of work, you know that?" Randy sighed. "Don't worry about Thanksgiving, obviously—and don't worry, period. I'll get it straightened out. Fairy-god-gay, at your service."

Mitch wanted to hug him, but he settled for a coffee-cup salute. "Thanks, Skeet."

Randy glanced at the closed bedroom door, heat coming back into his gaze. "So. You're going to be gone three days, and I'll be here alone with Peaches. What are the rules, Old Man?"

"Whatever he tells you."

Randy laughed. "God, you're so *cheesy*."

Happy, Mitch thought but didn't say, because now that they were in front of each other again, he could see that Randy wasn't.

"Rules are whatever he tells you he wants to do." Mitch rose and clapped his best friend on the shoulder. "Wouldn't mind getting some dirty pics on the road, though."

CHAPTER TWO

As the weekend of his arrival in Iowa unfolded, Randy Jansen digested the depth of quiet misery his friends had sunk into.

Only a little of Sam and Mitch's despair was because of work, school, and wedding stress, no matter how they tried to pass it off as such. Most of it was the acute torture that came with living in a small town. They could pretend they liked living here, that they had assimilated, but the truth was, they hadn't, and they weren't happy. And that made Randy unhappy.

They were sure pigheaded about the topic, though. When Randy tried to bring up the idea that perhaps this was not the perfect place for them after all, that maybe they should acknowledge Iowa's flaws, Mitch only said Middleton couldn't hold a candle to his hometown of McAllen, Texas, which, while true, didn't mean shit. Hell came in an assortment of shapes and sizes, most of it hating the fuck out of a rainbow.

It was clear, too, from watching Sam in the grocery store and at his favorite Mexican restaurant, that the carefree young man Randy knew in Las Vegas and on the road was someone else entirely in Middleton. Randy didn't care for this Sam: nervous, embarrassed of himself in a way that made it abundantly clear why he'd been so hesitant about his kink. Mitch wasn't as affected, but it was clear he too felt the pressure of a small town. Head down, out of the way, don't invite trouble.

Fuck. That.

Randy saw Mitch off on Sunday night, watched some bad TV with Peaches, and snuggled him in bed—without sex.

"I know he said it was okay to fool around without him here, but it feels like cheating to me." Sam blushed as he said this and looked up guiltily at Randy. "I'm sorry."

Randy kissed his forehead and held him

tight enough to let them feel each other's erections. "That's all right. I don't mind."

Sam sighed, settling into Randy's embrace. "Well, I think Mitch will. He wanted pictures. And don't forget he said point-blank on the way out the door he wanted some marks on my ass when he got back."

"Then I guess you'll have to let me bully you into baring your ass, won't you, and sending some naughty pics that don't involve me touching you. And I'll have to put the marks on you with a crop."

Sam shivered. "We don't have a crop, though. Mitch always uses his hands, because that's how I like it."

"I brought a crop *and* a cane in my carry-on." He pinched Sam's ass. "Mmm, that's going to make a nice picture. You with your pants down, the crop in your mouth. Looking up at the camera all desperate, your cock swinging."

Sam squirmed. "*Randy.*"

They did take exactly that picture, which Randy sent to Mitch with the added comment, *I also brought my cane.*

Mitch replied within fifteen minutes. *Pic*

with that next.

Randy sent Mitch several more pictures that night, and a video of him using the cane over Sam's jeans—then one last pic of Sam's reddened ass when they were done. Once Mitch got to a rest stop, Sam shooed Randy away and had a private Skype session with his fiancé, one that Randy could hear even when he went to stand on the balcony. He went to bed blue-balled beside a sore but sated Sam.

He didn't mind. He told himself he'd channel his sexual frustration into keeping his mind sharp, planning his attack.

He launched into it Monday morning, in total stealth. He fixed Sam breakfast and made jokes about sack lunches coming as soon as he could get to the store. Then he dropped Sam off at community college, waving and promising to pick him up at four thirty.

Once his charge was safely tucked away at school, Randy set off to unpack the nasty little town full of *good people* who liked to judge kinky boys.

He started with a self-guided tour, which didn't take long. The town was not much more than a postage stamp. Randy went through the downtown then followed the highway north to the high school. He drove out to Cherry Hill, which he knew from Sam was where his aunt and uncle lived. He scoped out the mini-mall, the farm implement store. When he spied the grocery, he parked and went inside, emerging forty-five minutes later with five cloth bags full of food. After a stop at the apartment to put everything away, he set an alarm to make sure he didn't miss Sam, and then he locked up the apartment and went, on foot, into the belly of the beast.

Downtown Middleton was, as far as Randy could tell, Mayberry. It was the sort of cute village he'd pined for as a kid until he got old enough to spy the cancer lurking beneath such places. The streets were tidy, the storefronts homey, but lift the lid and you found mold right away. Which was sad because there was real color and all kinds of potential in the town. Middleton was about fifteen thousand people, the county seat and a metropolitan hub for the stream of microscopic towns surrounding it. It had two high schools, public and private (Catholic), a community college, and a vibrant amateur theater. It had a coffee shop that whispered of hippies and book clubs.

The residents were, to Randy's surprise, not entirely white, but also Latino and a small representation of African-Americans. The ethnic groups didn't mix with each other, instead living in weird parallel versions of the town. Different neighborhoods, different streets for their businesses, different groups of kids loitering around parked cars or walking down the street.

The white people, no surprise, were the source of most of Middleton's skunkiness. They did their best to pretend it was 1950 or at least a world without competitive commerce: there was a furniture store where everything was overpriced as hell, a clothing store which was more of the same, and four kitschy antique stores. The proprietors regarded Randy suspiciously as he browsed their merchandise, though that was nothing compared to the tension when a person of color drifted inside. Smiles were reserved for Caucasians and people who could be in Tea

Party ads. Which meant the shop owners rarely smiled, because these patrons were few and far between.

Down side streets, however, were Latino stores that thrived. Randy discovered a Mexican grocery *and* a bakery, both overflowing with happy customers of all races chattering in Spanish and English. A Mexican general store with every sign in the window in Spanish clearly did brisk business as well. There were several Mexican restaurants and a bar, and the Latino businesses had young, aggressive shopkeepers welcoming anyone with money to spend.

The hub for angry old white people was the Middleton Cafe, which was retro-chic only because it hadn't once been updated, only the prices on the menus increasing. Randy spent an hour there reading *The Des Moines Register* and *The Middleton Herald Leader* as well as the *PennySaver* while he had an early lunch and eavesdropped. He heard an almost perfect robotic rehashing of the latest conservative talking points from one table, and some idealistic garbage from a pack of retired do-gooding liberals in a booth behind him. The whole room was nothing but theory and wishes about what was wrong with the world and how things could be fixed if people would only do this, that, or the other thing, or if so-and-so would die/get out of the way. The local newspaper was more of the same, and for that matter the opinion pages of *The Register* weren't much better. Everybody practiced armchair governance and revolution.

There wasn't a local Spanish paper, but the general store manager brightened when Randy spoke to him in Spanish and happily sold him a roaster for his Thanksgiving turkey, and the Mexican grocery provided him with some much-appreciated culinary comforts. Nobody talked about politics, though there were a few flyers for immigration rights lawyers and rallies.

Randy took note of the posters in the white stores too: most of them were school oriented, the rest from churches. He stopped by the two white bars on Main Street, where at the first one he had bad beer and deliberately lost three rounds of pool to a local retired vet missing his two front teeth and most of the buttons on his shirt. At the second pub, he pretended to give a shit about a talking-heads sports show and bought a round for the four third-shift meat-packing-plant workers decorating the stools. He eyeballed that establishment's flyers on the way out the door—local bands, mostly country, a veterans benefit, a fireman's pancake breakfast.

Yes, Middleton, Iowa, was pretty much what Randy had expected it to be. There was one place, though, he hadn't explored, and in many ways it was the most important recon yet. With several new friends and a significant lay of the land, Randy crossed the street to Biehl Drug, the store Sam's aunt and uncle owned.

It was small.

Randy hadn't expected the pharmacy to be a sprawling retail giant, and yet as he came through the door, the bell above his head tinkling to announce his arrival, all he could think of was that the place was tiny. Little, and so throwback it was almost creepy. A makeup counter—seriously, a makeup counter—stood to his right, and what had once been a soda fountain was on his left, now a display for electric razors, hairdryers, and curling irons. A glance at their stickers confirmed they were twice the price they would be at Walmart or any other store.

"May I help you?"

The woman who'd appeared at Randy's elbow was decidedly not Sam's famously sour-faced aunt Delia. The female next to him was young, bright-eyed, and smiling. Randy smiled back as he caught a glance at her name tag. "Emma. Yes, you most certainly can. I'm looking for some condoms."

She blinked, her smile not falling but growing more guarded. "Sure. I'll be happy to show you, sir."

Emma led him to the back of the store, and Randy took inventory as they walked. The floor squeaked under their feet, thin planks of polished wood that had to have been laid over one hundred years ago. Above his head suspended fluorescent fixtures buzzed, casting the narrow aisles in a sick yellow glow. A pungent bouquet of staleness and detergent assailed him, like a nursing home without the bodies. Silence rang about his ears, crowding out the hum of the bulbs. Ahead of him he saw the pharmacy counter, a raised dais walled off with fiberglass except for a narrow delivery/counseling station, filled with towering, crowded shelves and bathed in an even harsher, brighter set of overhead lights.

He tried to imagine Sam working here and shuddered.

The condoms were in a locked cabinet on the shelf just beneath the counter, and Emma had to ask the balding, white-coated man at the computer terminal to pass her a key. This would be Sam's uncle Norman, without question.

Emma unlocked the cabinet and pushed open the glass door. "Go ahead and help yourself."

The selection was paltry, and after watching Emma perform the dance of the lock, Randy assumed the pharmacy didn't sell condoms very often. How many people were brave enough to ask for prophylactics? Probably the only reason Biehl Drug carried them at all was because the single thing worse than having to sell condoms would be discovery as a less-than-full-service pharmacy.

Finding a brand and size that were adequate and rolling his eyes inwardly at the price markup, Randy slipped three packages off the metal peg. "Rather sad display of lubricants, Emma."

It was kind of fun, though depressing, how his essentially basic request for sexual paraphernalia flustered her. Wasn't Emma supposed to be Sam's designated fruit fly?

She glanced around the case as if seeing it for the first time. "Well, there's that tube of KY. Oh no. It's out of date. I'm sorry. I wonder if we have more in the back."

"That's all right. I'm not looking for *her pleasure* anyway. And while I'm giving you a critique of your sexual supplies, they're not always *family planning* aids." He pointed to the peeling label on the cabinet's rim.

She wasn't simply flustered now, she was awkward, clearly wishing Randy would go away and end her torment. "Um, sorry. I just work here."

This—*this*—was the woman who'd applauded Sam's alley fuck? Though as Randy recalled Sam's retelling of his journey from Middleton to Vegas, he remembered Emma was the friend who had tried, repeatedly, to call Sam home.

He rubbed his chin thoughtfully, trying to decide if he should explain who he was and give her a chance to defend herself. Except Randy started to wonder if Sam had even told Emma about him.

She smiled, the stretch of her lips declaring her someone who seriously wanted this confrontation over. "Is there anything else you needed, or should I ring you up?"

"Nope, pile of condoms ought to do it."

As she checked him out, Randy scanned her one more time, taking in the last few details that were her tell, and they made him sad. She wasn't a prude, and she had the trappings to let go and have fun, but she was, in so many ways, a symbol of all that held Sam back. As she totaled his purchases, engagement ring glinting in the overhead light, Randy could feel the hint of wildness before him taming under the weight of bridal catalogs and the promise of a house in a nice development, possibly with a whirlpool tub.

This, he reminded himself, was what Sam's wedding juxtaposed. This was the version of himself Sam couldn't have. Never mind Sam shouldn't want it. Emma didn't really want it either—but she wanted to belong. She wanted security and safety and solidity.

So long as Sam wanted to take it up the ass with another dick in his mouth instead of politely pounding a pussy, he couldn't belong. Not here. Not ever. Any wedding Sam planned in this environment wouldn't just be an also-ran. It would be nothing short of a total disaster.

"Emma, when you're finished with the customer, I need to see you in my office."

Randy turned toward the back of the pharmacy and saw a thin, pinch-faced woman with severe hair and cold, dead eyes looking back at him. She raked her gaze over Randy, mouth flattening in a line of disapproval.

Randy bit back a laugh. Sam's aunt, in the flesh. *Oh, Delia Biehl, it's lovely to meet you.*

He winked at Emma and picked up the brown paper bag—seriously, a stapled *brown paper bag*—with a flourish. "Thanks, sugar.

I'd say I'll think of you when I use them, but you're seriously not my type. Catch you around."

A ray of hope bloomed in him as Emma narrowed her eyes, dropping her reserve and studying him as if he were under a microscope. "Wait. Do I know you?"

"No, but we share a friend. I'll give Sam your love." He waved at the back of the pharmacy. "Stay sexy, Deils."

Randy strode out of the pharmacy, smiling as Delia sputtered indignantly behind him. He ambled up the street to the apartment, letting a plan unfold in his mind.

Sam and Mitch wanted to get married. Sam—hell, both of them—wanted to belong, but nobody could truly belong here. Middleton, Iowa, was a quiet anvil pressing slowly but effectively in the center of his best friends' chests, crushing out their joy.

But Sam *had* to get married in Iowa. Even if Nevada had marriage equality, Randy acknowledged that getting hitched in Sam's home state was a symbol for Sam, a kind of stepping stone before he bloomed in a brighter future.

It was going to take some research. It was going to take some time, and more than a little creativity. And it required one more minor yet crucial element.

Randy backtracked to the Mexican general store and stuck his head in, waving as the owner greeted him with a smile. "Hello again, sir. What can I do for you?"

Randy nodded at the bulletin board beside the cash register. "Do you happen to know of anybody looking to sell a car?"

CHAPTER THREE

MITCH HAD DONE Thanksgiving with Randy before, but he'd never had a Thanksgiving like this.

The food was pretty much what he'd expected. Well, he didn't know where, exactly, Randy had come up with half his ingredients and supplies, but it didn't surprise Mitch when he came home on Wednesday and discovered Sam wearing a dishtowel as an apron as he helped Randy prepare the turkey and put the finishing touches on the pies.

"Place smells amazing." Mitch noticed Randy didn't wear a dishtowel but had instead brought his own apron with him from Vegas, or had bought one somewhere on his excursions around town. This too didn't seem out of character in the slightest. He stepped between the two of them, goosing each of them on the ass. "Do I get dinner, or did you guys already eat?"

Sam flushed, looking guilty. "Oh, sorry, we made sandwiches earlier. I thought you'd eat on the road."

Normally Mitch would have, but he'd been too eager to get back to the boys. He winked at Sam. "Don't mind that. I'll find myself something."

Randy shook his head. "Settle down. I'll fix you a plate, but you need to help me wrestle this damn bird first. Go wash your hands and roll up your sleeves."

Mitch did as instructed, keeping one eye on Randy and Sam as they flopped the turkey carcass on the counter, struggling to get it out of its plastic wrapping, extricating the giblets. When his hands were dry, Randy jerked his head in the direction of a five-gallon bucket near the stove.

"Mitch, bring that over here and hold it just under the counter so we can wedge this inside."

Mitch obeyed, but he was a little bit mystified. "Why did you get such a big turkey? There's only three of us."

"Because turkey is the shit when I make it, as you well know, and this will freeze like nothing else. You'll eat like kings for months." Randy hefted the turkey and grunted against the weight. "Okay, Sam—you make sure the wings stay against the body as it goes in, got it?"

"Got it," Sam said, and in the bird went.

It fit neatly inside the blue plastic bucket, ass up and wings tucked to the sides. Once it was snug in that space and they'd all washed their hands, Randy had Sam pour in a bowl full of citrus, spices, and vegetables, and a *huge* amount of salt. Then they filled the thing with water almost to the top.

"Ah, you're brining it," Mitch realized.

Randy frowned. "Yes, but the dumb bitch is floating."

Sam held up a finger. "Hold on. I have an idea." He disappeared into the bedroom for a moment, then came back out with two of Mitch's five-pound weight discs, off the bar. "We could put these in a plastic gallon zip bag and set them on top. That ought to press the turkey down."

Randy ruffled his hair. "Thanks, Peaches.

Now all we have to do is play fridge Tetris and fit this bucket inside somehow."

It required a lot of creativity to rearrange everything in the refrigerator to make room for the turkey, especially since to fit the bucket they had to remove two shelves. Normally Mitch and Sam didn't have much in there, but Randy had chucked it full of things for his Thanksgiving prep and food in general.

"How many people you planning to feed this week?" Mitch shook his head as he took in the incredible amount of stuff Randy had procured. "I don't want to know what you spent."

"Not as much as you think. The Mexican grocery has great prices, and I cut a deal with the owner on a few things. Charm greases a lot of wheels." He wedged a carton of butter and a tub of sour cream into the last hole beside the bucket and shut the door. "All right. Sam, go give your lover a welcome home while I whip him up something."

Cheeks stained with a blush, Sam led Mitch by the hand to the couch. Mitch sat in the center, facing the kitchen, and Sam straddled his lap, smiling at him and touching his face, the collar of his shirt.

"How was your day?"

"Long." Mitch let out a breath as he drank in the sight of Sam, reading the signs of where they were headed, and his blood hummed. This was the fun of having Skeet around. For whatever reason, he saw to it Sam was always turned on, ready for sex at any second. He stroked the slender line of Sam's neck, stealing his fingers under Sam's shirt. "Couldn't wait to see you."

Sam smiled at him, the smile that made Mitch ache, the one he carried in his heart, the lighthouse that drew him home every day, no matter what bullshit he got tangled in. "I'm glad you have a few days off. That we both do—and that Randy's here too."

"Me too, Sunshine." Mitch trailed his touch down the center of Sam's chest, sliding over to find a nipple.

Something deep inside him began to purr when Sam gasped. Mitch massaged the nub, tugging it through the fabric. "You like that, baby?"

Sam nodded, working to keep his breathing even. "Yes, I do."

"Want me to keep going, mess with you more?" He brought his other hand to Sam's opposite nipple and began to draw on him in stereo. "Tell me what feels good, Sam."

Sam was already going under. "I like it when you pull on my tits like that." He whimpered and arched his back as Mitch tugged harder. "So good."

Mitch shot a glance at the kitchen to see if Randy was watching them as he made Mitch's dinner. He was. Mitch returned his attention to Sam, releasing his nipples. Before Sam had a chance to protest, Mitch said, "Take off your shirt, Sam."

Sam obeyed quickly, tossing it onto the arm of the couch. Once free of the garment, he put his hands behind his head, keeping his gaze fixed on Mitch, begging with his eyes.

Mitch didn't deny him. He resumed his slow, determined torture, able to get a better grip on his lover now without the shirt in the way. Mitch pinched the tender buds, turning them, pulling them away from Sam's body until he cried out in desperation.

It was so much fun. He could do it all

night. He had half a mind to do just that.

Except Sam's mewls were so exquisite, and his body quaked with such perfection, Mitch couldn't stand it. He had to push him further.

Letting go of Sam's left nipple, Mitch anchored his grip on Sam's hip and latched his mouth over the erect, aching nib.

Now when Sam cried out, Mitch felt the sound reverberating through his lover's body, buzzing against his lips as he sucked hard, making a seal around Sam's skin, teasing the sensitized bud with his tongue, grazing it against his teeth as he increased the suction. Sam all but sobbed as Mitch switched sides, crying out a plaintive, "No, no, *no*," as Mitch began to pinch the tortured, wet left nubbin.

When Mitch switched sides again, Sam sank into despair, but he didn't use his safe word, only turned into a stiff sheet in Mitch's arms as he endured.

A shadow fell over them. "Your dinner's ready, Old Man."

Mitch lifted his head, wiping a trail of saliva from his chin. He had to hold a quavering Sam up with both hands now. "Thanks. You want to take over this business for me?"

"*No.*" Sam covered his face.

Randy grinned a terrible grin. "Be happy to."

Randy had fixed Mitch an omelet with leftover ham, some peppers, onions, and mushrooms. It was fantastic, but it was difficult to focus on it with the show that came with his meal. Whereas Mitch had kept Sam on his lap, Randy spread him out on the coffee table, which he quickly figured out had handy hidden straps for tying someone down. He immobilized Sam's wrists, then went to town on him, licking a long, wicked line from his bellybutton to his chin, teasing fingers across his chest, touching everywhere but on Sam's nipples. When he added featherlight touches at Sam's groin as well, Sam came unglued.

"*Please, Randy.*" He was nearly crying.

Randy sat on his haunches, patient, stroking Sam as if he had all the time in the world. "What is it you want me to do, sugar?"

"I want you to *touch me.*"

"Baby, I'm doing nothing but touch you. Be more specific."

Mitch grinned around his fork. He always forgot how mean Randy could be.

Sam whimpered and fought against his restraints. "Get me off, Randy, *please*. I'll do anything."

Mitch raised his eyebrows and sat back, meal forgotten. Oh, this was going to be *good*.

"Anything, hmm?" Randy palmed Sam's aching bulge. "How about…I'll let you get off, but you let me cane you first."

It was a sign of how wound up Sam was that he agreed without hesitation. All week while Mitch had been on the road and they'd sent him pics or he'd talked to Sam on the phone, Randy had been teasing him with that cane, and Sam had been having none of it, not after that first night when he'd experienced how hard it hurt even through clothes. Mitch caught Randy's gaze and raised an eyebrow.

Randy shook his head. "It'll be fine. We've been working up to it. I convinced him you'd enjoy it. He wanted it to be a surprise for you."

Okay, *now* Mitch was turned on. He pushed away the last of his omelet and settled in. "The surprise is appreciated. And I'm enjoying myself already."

Randy undid Sam's wrists and helped him stand on his shaking legs, leading him to the bedroom, motioning for Mitch to follow. "Not out here. I have this all worked out. You're going to sit at the head of the bed, and he's going to drape over your lap. This way you get the best show possible. And our boy gets the softness of the bed and the security of you petting him while I go after his backside."

It was indeed a damn good show, with Sam naked and ass-up over Mitch's legs, squirming and whimpering, holding on to Mitch's hand as Randy got ready. Mitch was turned on as hell, but he couldn't help checking in with Sam.

"Sunshine, you can say no."

"I know." Sam's breath was raspy, shaking. "I don't want to. I want to do this." He held tight to Mitch. "I want you with me, though."

So that was how Mitch watched Sam get his first caning: deeply moved and hard as a Texas brick. Randy didn't whip him nearly as intensely as he could have, Mitch couldn't help but notice. There would be some nice stripes, yes, but they'd be pink at best and wouldn't last more than a day. Sam wouldn't have much trouble sitting down. Though Sam wasn't much for sharp pain, which Skeet knew. It was mostly the idea that he was doing this thing that scared him, doing it for Mitch.

They got him off good after, Mitch from the front, kissing and grinding against him while Randy rutted at his backside. They came in a sweaty mess of bodies that meant Mitch would be changing the sheets. Randy wouldn't let him, though—told him to get Sam showered and he'd do it. So Mitch made out with Sam under the spray and kept him awake long enough to pour him into the crisp linens once they were finished.

Afterward, he sat up and played some cards and drank with Randy until his eyelids were drooping too, at which point he climbed in beside Sam. He heard Randy getting settled in the spare room, tossing and turning on the air mattress, and then the next thing he knew it was morning and the house was full of wonderful smells, the kitchen bustling with

Randy and Sam putting together the final dishes for the meal.

The food was, of course, incredible. There was enough turkey for half the town, Mitch was sure of it, except when the three of them were finished, there was a lot less left than he would have guessed.

They put the leftovers in the fridge, and then the three of them did the dishes together. Randy teased Sam and got him to blush, then egged Mitch on and made him swat Randy in the ass with a towel. It was, in short, the perfect end to a perfect day.

Except then Mitch found out the fun wasn't over.

Randy pulled his pumpkin and apple pies from where they were chilling on the balcony, and grabbed forks from the drawer and a tub of freshly made whipped cream from the fridge. "Time for dessert."

Mitch didn't think he had a single inch of room, but the sight of those pies had his brain correcting his stomach's misconceptions. "I'll get the plates."

"Oh, don't bother. We don't need any plates." Randy smiled at Sam with the devil's grin, backing him slowly toward the coffee table. "We're using Peaches as our plate."

Sam looked equal parts terrified and turned on, and Mitch corrected himself once more.

He wasn't simply hungry for that pie now. He was *ravenous*.

CHAPTER FOUR

IT WASN'T UNTIL the Friday after Thanksgiving that Mitch found out Randy had cancelled his flight back to Vegas.

"You need me here," Randy said with a shrug when Mitch asked him why. He'd made scrambled eggs with cheese, onion, peppers—real hot peppers that made Mitch's belly burn happily—and bacon. Randy spooned a healthy portion onto Mitch's plate. "So I'm staying."

"What, you're just going to move in?" Mitch forked a bite of egg, and pleasure rippled through him as he put the food in his mouth.

"For now, but not for long." Randy flicked Mitch's sleeve with his fork. "Don't worry, I won't get too comfy."

"That's not what I meant." Mitch took

another bite and groaned. "Fuck, Skeet. The shit you do to food."

"Yes, if only some rich sugar daddy would put me up in a designer kitchen. Think of how fat I could make him." Randy sipped his coffee and leaned back in his chair. "Old Man, having been here a week, I'm here to tell you this shit is a mess. It's more than schedules and money and poor queers who can't go to the ball. You need to get out of this stinking-thinking you two have going on. I know you can't move until Sam's done with school, but the second that happens, you need to get the hell out of Dodge. Until that time, you need to do your damnedest to crawl outside of the fucking box this town has you in."

Mitch frowned. "What do you mean?"

"I mean this place has been your home base for how long now, and you've made exactly zero friends. Sam's BFF has potential, but she's got her head up her own skirt."

Mitch had gotten an earful from Sam about how Randy had tested Emma. "You could have been a little less bull-in-a-pharmacy with her from what I was told."

"Yes, I could have. But I wanted a read on

her, and I got one. She's a nice girl who'll have a vibrator in her bedside drawer until she has kids and she hides it in the back of her bureau and forgets about it, content to have sex once a month—if that—quick in the dark so the kids don't hear. That's about as deep as she goes. And outside of you, she's Sam's single, solitary close friend here. She most likely went to her sweetie's family yesterday for the holiday and tittered over how they were making love in his childhood bedroom. Meanwhile Peaches wore a vibrating plug and a ball gag and let us eat pumpkin pie and whipped cream off his abdomen before we gang-banged him over the back of the couch. It's bad enough *you're* holing up and waiting for your prison sentence to be over, but you have to remember: Sam doesn't know Middleton is jail. He thinks this is normal. We gotta get him to some actual kink-loving normal. STAT."

Randy had a point. Mitch ran a hand over his face and sighed. "I'd take him on the road more, get him out to Vegas, but with his school—"

"Jesus. *No,* you can't take him out of here

to find it. He's got to feel normal *here*. He needs—fuck, *you* need—to learn how to feel normal any-fucking-where you land." When Mitch started to protest, Randy waved his sputter away airily. "I know you don't know how to do that. This is why I cancelled my flight. I can play online poker and go to casinos and work on cars as easily here as I can back home. It's just colder here and more boring." He glanced at the clock on the wall. "Speaking of cars. We need to finish up here so I can go pick up mine."

"You bought a car?"

"Van, technically, but yes. I need a way to get around. This one-car bullshit in a town with no public transportation is for the birds. If Sam were at school this morning instead of work, one of us would've had to drive him or we'd be without a vehicle." Randy grinned around a bite of egg. "It's an old conversion van all tricked out. Needs carburetor work, and exhaust. Gonna work at it in Mario's brother's garage, which'll hopefully lead to repair jobs. But if not, there's always online poker."

"Who's Mario?"

"Guy who owns the Mexican grocery store. He's looking out for me, and in exchange, I'm doing some work for him."

Mitch tried to digest it all, but mostly he kept hanging up on the fact that he wasn't taking Randy back to the airport on Sunday. He was waking up to eggs and hash browns and coming home to meatloaf and a clean house and fucking Sam with him. Every day.

They got the van, and they tinkered with it in the alley until Sam got home. Over dinner, Randy shared his announcement about staying, and Sam's joy made Mitch's heart swell even as he felt guilty. He should have seen this, known what Sam needed without being told.

"That's not how it works," Randy said when Mitch confessed as much as they did dishes together. "You can't see stuff like that in your own day-to-day. If you dropped into my life and poked around, you'd see all kinds of things I'm missing."

"I wouldn't see it like you do. And I probably wouldn't know how to fix it."

"So then you be glad I *do* see so well and am a manipulative bossy-pants who will help you scheme to a happily ever after."

Mitch glanced at the couch, where Sam sat with headphones as he pored over a reading assignment. "I thought I already got that. The happy ever after, I mean."

"Yeah, well, that's where you're wrong, Old Man. You don't just ride Old Blue into the sunset and call it good. You keep on driving, into one hot mess after another." He swatted Mitch on the butt with the dishtowel. "Be glad I'm here to help steer you back onto the road when you go off course."

Mitch *was* glad. He really, really was.

RANDY HAD BEEN looking for wedding venues since before he'd arrived in Iowa, but after his Thanksgiving-week recon, he had a second and far more crucial mission: finding Sam and Mitch some local kink.

He knew from Sam's stories of his pre-Mitch past how he'd had a string of regular tricks—straight boys he'd blow in the bathroom, a regular fuck-buddy who turned Sam's crank with his disinterest—but Randy also knew that since Sam's return to his hometown, his kink was with Mitch, and multiple partners happened only on the road. When asked about this, Sam stammered and blushed and said he didn't have time. Mitch, when the two of them were alone, said he knew what Randy was getting at and agreed, but his intense driving schedule had meant it was hard to get out and vet potential candidates.

He also made it clear he'd be grateful if Randy put that task on his to-do list. So Randy did.

Grindr options were thin on the ground but better than Randy had thought they would be, and in addition to several prospects for a friendly orgy, he got to be pounded in the men's restroom of one of the bars by a burly top with a thick beard and thicker cock. What Randy had trouble finding, though, were younger men. He wasn't sure why his instincts kept steering him into that pool, but they did, so he went with it. There were plenty of sweet young things looking for a good time, and Randy gave a few of them what they sought, but they were too friendly, and all bottoms. Sam needed a bossy, angry top to call him a slut and mean it, and Mitch needed to watch. This was a tough order to fill.

Well—okay. Amend that. Randy didn't know how to fill it and still keep Sam safe, physically and mentally. Yes, Mitch would be there to guard him, and initially so would Randy, but he wasn't having anyone make his Peaches feel crappy about his fetish. It was not the case that just anyone would do. Problem was, Randy was beginning to feel nobody would do.

Then one night Randy met Keith Jameson at the bar, and he laughed at himself for taking so long to see what was right in front of him the whole time.

Keith was, Randy knew, Sam's favorite straight-boy hookup at school, and given the amount of tit-watching the guy engaged in, straight was very much what Keith was. But an evening's observation told Randy something else—Keith liked rough trade more than he liked tits and pussy. There was an edge to him, a need to fuck hard and spew venom at his partner, a yen born not out of hatred but a dark vein of forbidden. Randy would bet serious money this guy had a computer full of hard-core porn back at his apartment. This was why he liked to fuck Sam's mouth in the school bathroom. What a rush that must have been, subjugating someone who wanted it so much.

Odds were good the guy hadn't had anyone like Sam since Sam.

Smiling around the edge of his drink, Randy decided it was time poor Keith had a shift in fortune.

Flirting with a straight guy was an art Randy had perfected long ago. There were men nobody could touch with a ten-foot pole, but they were few and far between. Most people liked attention, and nearly all men loved sex. When Randy had a straight fish in his sights, he bought him a drink, chatted him up, and laid his groundwork. Keith was no exception, and it didn't take long to find the lure: when Keith found out Randy lived in Vegas, he was all ears. Randy told him everything he wanted to know: about the Nevada brothels, about sex parties, about the lure of a constant stream of random strangers.

Eventually Randy moved them to a table in the back of the bar with a pitcher of Pabst, under the guise of telling Keith even filthier tales. He did—but it wasn't long before the stories were rather gay. They always featured Randy, though—Randy letting guys do things to him and loving it. He told a lot of stories about fucking straight guys and letting them fuck him.

"Sex is sex, right?" He leaned back in his chair and ran the toe of his boot along Keith's ankle. "Best fun sometimes is with a guy who isn't actually into me. Sometimes it's good to be used. And nobody uses you like a straight man."

He gave Keith a blowjob in the alley—it was a little chilly, but Keith gave good hair-pull. They exchanged numbers, and it wasn't long before Randy was making regular visits to Keith's apartment to get the shit fucked out of him. It pleased him to be the kid's first gay fuck. He taught the guy how to set up a Grindr account and assured him it was more than fine to say he was a straight guy only wanting to fuck and get sucked, no favors returned.

"Bigger kink than you might be thinking," he promised.

Keith really was a nice guy, especially once someone let him go raw on their ass. "There used to be this guy at school. But he's dating somebody now, and he's not interested."

God, Randy loved it when a game went the way he wanted it to. "Would this be Sam Keller?"

Keith's eyes widened in surprise. "How did you know?"

Randy's grin was feral. "Let me tell you a *few more* stories, sugar."

When he went back to Sam and Mitch's place that night, his ass was sore, his jaw hurt, and he was ready to fuck Sam like nobody's business. Mitch saw what was coming as soon as Randy walked in the door and went for the rope. He took Sam's books out of his hand, stripped him naked, and tied his wrists above his head. Randy spread Sam, lifted his ass with a pillow, and worked him open with a clinical efficiency that made Sam wriggle and moan.

"Got you a present." Randy got a third

finger into Sam's ass, burrowing to his knuckles. "Somebody's coming over tomorrow night. You're going to suck him off, I'm teaching him how to paddle you, and then he's doing you while we watch."

Sam's gaze went dark, a beautiful mix of fear and anticipation. "Oh?"

"Yeah." Randy pushed Sam's legs open wider and admired the gape before going in again. "He's straight, but he likes rough sex and loves using. We've been meeting up all week, and he's excited to do you. He'll twist your shame kink until you burst." Randy pulled out of Sam, slipped on a condom, and drove inside hard enough to make Sam stutter for breath. "Best part is, you've already been with him. He says he misses your mouth."

Sam's eyes flew open. "Randy, who— *Ungh.*" Sam shut his eyes and moved his hips in time to Randy's thrusts.

Randy bent down and ran a wet tongue down the side of Sam's ear. "Keith Jameson."

Sam cried out in alarm, and Randy laughed against his neck and fucked Peaches until he shuddered and came.

Once recovered, Sam began to protest, saying he couldn't do it, he didn't want Keith to fuck him—except it was obvious as hell that he did. Mitch took point, making Sam give him a blowjob, then turning him, still tied, onto his stomach and doing him hard and rough as he whispered in Sam's ear how much he was looking forward to seeing Keith take a shot at him. Randy had mastered the mimic of Sam's favorite porn thrust weeks ago, and they'd spent many a night with Randy snapping and rolling his hips as he pounded Sam into the mattress while Mitch looked on.

They didn't let Sam come a second time, and in fact they spent the better part of that night and the next morning, until Sam had to go to work, ramping him up. When he got home, they started up again, never letting him get off, always whispering about how good it would be to see him with Keith.

"He's been fucking me for days." Randy stroked Sam's dick and licked his ear as he teased him. "Grabs my hair and *yanks* that shit while he stuffs that monster into my mouth." He nipped Sam's earlobe. "Bet you miss that big snake in your throat. Bet you remember. *He* remembers. Said nobody whimpered like you when he fucked their face. Said you were the best."

Sam whimpered now, squirming against Randy, his eyes darting always over to Mitch.

When Keith finally showed up, it was hard to say who was hornier or more anxious, Sam or the boy who'd come to fuck him. Keith hovered in the doorway, looking ready to bolt if anyone breathed on him funny, and Sam stayed near Mitch, watching Keith like a hawk but not letting go of his fiancé's arm. Mitch kept a close eye on Sam, but he also shot plenty of *don't you upset my boy* glances at Keith.

Jesus, what a mess.

Randy assessed the situation, let them all fuck with each other for a few minutes, then clapped his hands. "All right, boys. I think we could all do with a few medicinal rounds of mescal, don't you?"

He lined up four glasses on the counter and poured two fingers into each, launching into teasing mode as they got the liquid down. He wasn't going to let anyone get drunk, but loose was definitely going to be an advantage here. Mitch arrived at relaxed first, taking a Bohemia from the fridge as he assumed his position in his chair for the show, and Keith's shoulders settled into a more comfortable plane as he finished his glass and leaned against the fridge.

That only left Sam, and Randy knew what to do with him. Putting his drink aside, Randy leaned on the counter and pointed at the floor in front of him. "Peaches, get on your knees and suck my dick."

Sam blushed, glancing around the room, his gaze lingering on Keith. Then he let out a shuddering sigh, finished off the last of his mescal, and got on the floor in front of Randy. His fingers trembled as he undid Randy's belt and button, but as he set Randy's semihard erection free, Sam began to calm.

Not all the way, though. He turned his head to look at Keith, who was still standing at the fridge.

Randy gripped his hair and forced his attention back to his dick.

"*My* dick, honey. I know you're greedy for Keith's cock, that you want him to treat you miss that big snake in your throat. Bet you remember. *He* remembers. Said nobody whimpered like you when he fucked their face. Said you were the best."

Sam whimpered now, squirming against Randy, his eyes darting always over to Mitch.

When Keith finally showed up, it was hard to say who was hornier or more anxious, Sam or the boy who'd come to fuck him. Keith hovered in the doorway, looking ready to bolt if anyone breathed on him funny, and Sam stayed near Mitch, watching Keith like a hawk but not letting go of his fiancé's arm. Mitch kept a close eye on Sam, but he also shot plenty of *don't you upset my boy* glances at Keith.

Jesus, what a mess.

Randy assessed the situation, let them all fuck with each other for a few minutes, then clapped his hands. "All right, boys. I think we could all do with a few medicinal rounds of mescal, don't you?"

He lined up four glasses on the counter and poured two fingers into each, launching into teasing mode as they got the liquid down. He wasn't going to let anyone get drunk, but loose was definitely going to be an advantage here. Mitch arrived at relaxed first, taking a Bohemia from the fridge as he assumed his position in his chair for the show, and Keith's shoulders settled into a more comfortable plane as he finished his glass and leaned against the fridge.

That only left Sam, and Randy knew what to do with him. Putting his drink aside, Randy leaned on the counter and pointed at the floor in front of him. "Peaches, get on your knees and suck my dick."

Sam blushed, glancing around the room, his gaze lingering on Keith. Then he let out a shuddering sigh, finished off the last of his mescal, and got on the floor in front of Randy. His fingers trembled as he undid Randy's belt and button, but as he set Randy's semihard erection free, Sam began to calm.

Not all the way, though. He turned his head to look at Keith, who was still standing at the fridge.

Randy gripped his hair and forced his attention back to his dick.

"*My* dick, honey. I know you're greedy for Keith's cock, that you want him to treat you rough in front of us, but you're *my* hole right now." He yanked on Sam's hair and slapped his cock against the side of Sam's face. "Suck this, bitch. Make it hard. Open that hole and show me what it's for."

Whimpering, Sam opened his mouth wide and turned his head toward Randy's dick, trying to trap it inside.

Randy slid into the offered opening, teasing the ring, then sliding in over Sam's tongue. "There you go. Good hole. Now seal it up, Hole. That's right. And suck it. Suck while I push into your throat." He pressed in far enough to make Sam gag a little. "Suck harder." He pushed against the back of Sam's throat a few times, making him cry and whimper—he glanced at Sam's right hand and made sure he had his handkerchief on him, and he did—then he pulled out, just past Sam's puffy lips dripping with saliva. Then he drove in again, right to the back, thrusting and ordering Sam to suck harder until he was gurgling and almost crying.

After a few rounds of that he gave Sam a break, switching to shallow fucks inside his mouth as he anchored himself on Sam's hair, and he turned to Keith, who had been watching the entire show with a feral look in his eye.

Randy winked at him. "We've taught Sam a lot since you last had his mouth. But you knew about the hair-pulling, right?" Randy yanked hard on Sam's hair, making Sam moan and suck harder. "The more you yank, the harder he sucks. And you can deep throat this slut like nothing else. Really bang in there. Here, Peaches—show him how you let me face-fuck you. Not the slow stuff we've been doing or the deep holds. Let me pound you."

Sam, gasping for air around Randy's cock, looked worn out and wrecked, but not terrified. He also looked slutty as fuck and turned on as hell. He nodded at Randy and opened his mouth wide.

Randy massaged his hair. "That's right. Open up. Little more. Nice and wide. Give me a good hole. But stop looking at Keith. Look at me." He slapped Sam's cheek. "Up. That's the way. Right in my eyes. Gonna fuck your throat open. Shoot my load down so Keith can watch. Mitch too. You've been waiting a long time for this. You want Mitch to see the guy you were slutty with first. Feel all that shame rolling around while a straight boy from home fucks your face, then your ass."

Keith moved closer, his expression hungry. "Shit, he lets you talk to him like that?"

Randy snorted. "Honey, he loves it. Don't you, Peaches? You love it when I call you a slut. Because you are a slut. Aren't you?" He pulled out of Sam's mouth and pinched his nipple through his shirt, hard enough to make Sam wince. "Tell him. Tell Keith you're a slut. Look him in the eye and tell him."

Cheeks burning red, Sam turned his head and looked Keith in the eye. "I'm a slut."

Randy tugged at the nipple he'd captured. "Tell him you like getting fucked in the mouth by strangers."

Shame radiated from Sam like heat. "I like getting fucked in the mouth by strangers."

Randy wouldn't let up. "And how do you feel about men you barely know fucking you and treating you roughly in front of your fiancé?"

They might as well have peeled off Sam's skin, he was so raw. "I want it so much I could get off just thinking about it."

"Shall we let you have that, then?" Randy stepped closer and ran the tip of his dick along Sam's cheek. "Shall I teach Keith how to use you and treat you rough?"

Sam shuddered, closed his eyes. "Yes, *please*."

"Then turn back to me and open, baby. And be a good, good slut, and show us all how much you want this."

Sam did. Face flaming with shame, eyes banked with lust, he opened his mouth and held still while Randy pounded into his throat, moving fast and rough but then sometimes going deep and holding himself in there until Sam gagged, then pulling back and fucking deep again. Randy deliberately kept tripping that gag reflex, and every time Sam gagged, Keith stiffened and dug his fingers into his jeans. When Randy came, he pulled out and sprayed all over Sam's face, and Sam kept his mouth open like a baby bird, letting his tongue coat with cum.

Keith had his dick out before Randy had his put away—he gripped Sam's hair and drove in, and with a moan, Sam took him home.

It really was a sight—Keith was a motherfucker, swearing at Sam and calling him names as he thrust and demanded Sam suck harder. He pulled his hair until he cried out, which of course only made Sam wilder.

Randy knelt behind Sam, nibbling on his neck while Keith fucked his face and Randy undid his pants. "Gonna bare your ass, because it's next. Let Keith see how hard this gets you. How the more names he calls you and the rawer he gets, the harder you are. Sweet little slut. Show him how much you missed this cock in your mouth, how much you want it in your ass."

Sam showed him. Sam sucked him and whimpered and looked up adoringly at Keith while he spewed venom. Keith came on his face, drawing Sam's head down to let the spunk hit his hair.

With a wicked laugh, Randy pinched Keith's ass, then led Sam to the couch for round two.

It was in so many ways one of Randy's all-time favorite sex adventures with Sam and Mitch. Randy got to drive, but it was performance all the way—for Mitch, who simply sat in his armchair, dark gaze observing; for Keith, who willingly took up every raunchy act Randy egged him into. Randy opened Sam on his lap, encouraging Keith to watch while Randy greased Sam up. "Making him ready for you. All spread, getting himself wet." He tweaked Sam's nipple with lube-slick fingers. "You want to get wetter for Keith, Peaches? You want to be so wet you drip for him?"

Sam groaned, shut his eyes, and drew his legs wider.

Randy worked him with so much lube it slid from him as Keith arranged him on the coffee table, braced on a pile of cushions.

Randy held him down while Keith got ready behind him, pinching Sam's nipples.

"You're just a hole tonight, Sam, a slutty series of holes. He used the first one, and now he's after this one. Let him see it." Randy smacked Sam's ass with his hand, then continued to tug ruthlessly on Sam's nipple as he spoke to Keith. "What do you think of the hole? Open wide enough? Wet enough? Would you like to fuck it now, play with it? Push things into it? Slap it?"

Keith stilled. "Slap it?"

Sam whimpered, burying his face in his hands. "*No*, please."

Randy slapped his ass again, then, out of spite, moved behind him and gave him a sharp slap against his perineum and over his waiting hole. Sam cried out and shivered, but ultimately didn't move. Randy nodded in satisfaction and turned to Keith.

"Slap it. Like that." He slapped Sam again, several times in succession, making him gasp and squirm and beg for Randy to stop. He didn't, not until Sam whimpered and pushed against him desperately. "He loves to hate that one. You can mix it up too. Sharp slaps until he's compliant, finger-fuck him until he's desperate, then slap him again. Call him a dirty slut the whole time. Then out of nowhere start fucking him. Rough and hard until you're done."

The expression on Keith's face was dark and dangerous and delightful. "How about slapping his ass and thighs. And pinching them."

"Fair game, within reason. If he calls out *violet* or drops that red hanky, it's over, or if

Mitch or I tell you to stop, you stop. Otherwise no matter what he tells you, you keep going. In fact, if he begs you to stop without the word violet and that hanky is still in his hand, you go to fucking town, buddy. Got it?"

Keith grinned and stroked his dick. "Yeah. Got it."

Keith got it all right. He played with Sam like a spider toying with a fly. First he mimicked Randy's play, slapping at Sam and fingering him, but then he began to fuck him, slapping and pinching whatever flesh he could find as he pounded away. He loved going hard, loved a rough scene. He used Sam mercilessly, until Sam was crying and begging him to stop—at which point Keith only laughed and went harder.

Yet, as the night progressed, as Randy led them into other games, the three of them together, always, he couldn't help but notice Jameson's hard edges were rubbing off. He began to show a strange kind of affection for what he was allowed to do to Sam, speaking almost reverently about pounding Sam's ass.

"He's so amazing," he whispered to Randy when Mitch and Sam were reconnecting in the bedroom alone and Keith and Randy were getting water in the kitchen. "I mean—I always knew he gave great head, and he seemed like a nice guy otherwise, but holy crap, the guy can take a pounding. I would be in tears over what he's been through. And you're telling me he's just resting?"

Randy smiled around his glass. "He won't rest until Mitch has had him too. And he'll want you to see that. His way of letting you know that was all fun and games, but at the end of the day, Mitch is the one for him."

"Well I *know* that," Keith protested.

Randy shook his head. "It's not about knowing. It's about showing."

Once the break was over, Randy trussed Peaches to a bench, shoved a metal plug in deep, strapped all his appendages down, and taught Keith how to paddle him. He taught him, too, how to take Sam all the way to the edge of coming but not let him get there, showed Keith what a fun head-fuck that was. Sam began to alternate between whimpering about his ass and begging to get off. He wasn't allowed, though, not until Keith had fucked him over the bench, followed by Randy. With spent condoms littered at his knees and five loads coating his body, Sam, still hard as a bar of iron, went limp everywhere else as Randy untied him and laid him out like an offering for Mitch.

Keith watched, quiet, as Mitch fucked his fiancé more ruthlessly than Randy or Keith had. He noted, Randy knew, the difference between Sam getting fucked to get off and Sam getting fucked by the man he loved, however roughly. When Sam came, Keith shuddered. As Sam and Mitch retreated into the bathroom and then to bed, Randy passed Keith the bottle of mescal and a glass.

"You know," Randy said once they'd both had a shot, "there are girls who will let you fuck them like that too."

Keith shut his eyes and sank back into the couch. "I don't know how the hell to find them."

"Look. That's how. Get out there. Put yourself out there—but be smart. Remember, with girls or guys you've got to be more delicate when you first meet them so they know you're not a psycho. Too many guys are asses, and they'll be checking to see if you're going to fuck them up in a bad way. Letting someone use you like this takes trust. And when it's someone of your actual orientation, reciprocate. With girls, a little cunnilingus never goes amiss."

Keith snorted and took another hit of mescal. "Hanging out with gay men isn't going to teach me that."

"Please. If I weren't so tired, I'd go find a girl and show you right now." When Keith's jaw fell open, Randy rolled his eyes. "What, you think you're the only one in the world who loves sex enough not to be particular about how he gets it? I'm not straight, not even bi, but man do women come apart nice when you seduce them right."

Keith stared at Randy like he wanted to blow him. It pleased Randy to know he could probably make that happen. "Would—would you show me? Seriously?"

Randy put an arm around Keith's shoulders. "Oh, sweetheart. I thought you'd never ask."

CHAPTER FIVE

MITCH RARELY SAW Randy during the month of December. Randy spent plenty of time at a local garage owned by the brother of the guy who ran the Mexican grocery, putzing with cars and trucks and telling dirty jokes in his bad Spanish. He kept the house cleaner than a hospital emergency room, and there was always a pile of food in the kitchen. Even if he was gone for a few days, he left casseroles and storage containers in the freezer with notes on the front of the fridge explaining how everything should be prepared.

Randy left Middleton sometimes for days at a time, usually playing poker, though he said he was also wedding planning—in part because his poker playing fueled his van and provided his slush fund for deposits. He was furious when he learned he couldn't play online in Iowa, and Mitch suspected Skeet or his gangster friend in Vegas discovered a workaround. Mostly, though, Randy hit the live games at casinos across the state, as well as a few private ones. He favored the Horseshoe in Council Bluffs, but he went just as often to Prairie Meadows in Altoona, a few miles east of Des Moines. After a few weeks, Randy had Mitch drop him off when he was going on a quick run in the right direction, having Mitch pick him up on the way home. Poker games went well into the wee hours of the morning, and Skeet liked to get on board Old Blue after a breakfast at the casino buffet and sleep all the way back to Middleton.

He wasn't only gambling, though. Randy wouldn't give any details, but he was constantly spinning out plans for the wedding, asking Sam and Mitch what their preferences were on style and substance and sometimes finer details about setting. One night shortly before Christmas, he fed them Christmas cookies and rum-heavy eggnog and grilled them but good.

"What would you do for a wedding if you

could do anything?" He pulled Sam into a straddle over his lap and trailed fingers down the center of his chest. "If you had a fairy godmother, what would you wish for? A trip to Aruba? Debauchery? Fairy tale?"

Sam, who was significantly tipsy, smiled wistfully instead of giving his usual response of closing off and insisting the wedding didn't matter. "I want a pretty ceremony and something fun after. I don't care about the theme. I like the idea of all kinds of people there who are happy for me. I don't want a church, but I'd want the ceremony to be meaningful." He slipped his fingers into Randy's hair in a clumsy gesture. "The reception should be fun, though. A big party."

Randy ran his hands over Sam's ass, slipping his fingers under his waistband. "Dirty party?"

"Maybe." Sam's wicked smile faded into naked sorrow. "Except nobody's gonna come to my wedding *or* my reception, Randy, except you and Em. I don't even think Keith would come."

"Hush." Randy swatted him on the butt and turned to Mitch. "What about you, Old

Man? What's your dream wedding? And you can't say whatever Sam wants. That's copping out, and it's rude. Fess up. What is it you wish you could do when you get hitched?"

Mitch sipped his eggnog and ate another cookie as he considered. For so long he hadn't thought he'd ever get married, period, let alone have a ceremony to wish over. But Randy wanted an answer, and a glance at Sam said his lover did too.

"Valentine's Day," Mitch said at last. "I'd want to get married on Valentine's Day."

He expected teasing, but Randy only smiled an enigmatic smile, and Sam climbed off Randy's lap and onto Mitch's, his expression puppy-dog sweet. "Oh, Mitch, that's so romantic. I think we should do that. Even if we just go down to the courthouse, we should get married on Valentine's Day."

Mitch raised an eyebrow at Randy. "Does that work with the plans you're making? Valentine's Day isn't very far away."

Randy rolled his eyes. "Hooker, I could throw you a gala in twenty minutes with one hand tied behind my back and a cock rammed down my throat. V-day it is." He scooted closer on the couch and ran a hand down Sam's leg. "But speaking of cock, I'd like to put mine in your butt, baby."

As he always did, Sam went soft and glassy at the prospect of getting done. They'd had Keith over several times, and Mitch suspected long after Randy went home *that* particular carnival ride would keep spinning, but there was something special about it being the three of them, the original triad, playing a game. They did Sam right there, working his jeans down with him still kneeling over Mitch's lap. Randy greased Sam and made a big show of using one of the Biehl drugstore condoms, kissing Sam's neck as he murmured wickedly against his skin.

"I'll have to go down tomorrow and tell them we've used up all the condoms." He nipped the fleshy lobe of Sam's ear. "Tell them how much I enjoyed them. I'll make sure you're there too, so you blush and they realize I used *family planning devices* on you."

Sam shut his eyes with a delicious shiver. Mitch caught his cock and drew his attention back, skimming his other hand up Sam's chest to tweak a nipple.

"Tell me what Randy's doing to you, Sunshine." He pulled the nipple taut. "Look me in the eye and tell me everything."

Sam's gaze was hooded, lust-dark, his tongue loosened but words sludgy because of the alcohol. "He has his fingers in me."

Mitch slapped Sam's flank. "More specific."

Sam quivered. Mitch could see the muscle of Randy's arm, his eyes glittering as he sucked all around Sam's shoulder.

"F-fingers." Sam anchored himself on Mitch's arm. "A…couple. Moving. In and out. Biting my shoulder. Sucking it."

"Yep. He's gonna leave marks all over. And I'm gonna mark your ass after he fucks it. Is he fucking you now? What's he doing with those fingers?"

Sam kept gasping, hips jerking as Randy worked him. "Twisting. Pushing—*ohgod.*"

Mitch twisted too, renewing his attack on Sam's nipples. This was what Mitch liked, Sam flustered and on the edge. Nobody rode shame like Sam. Nobody dutifully reported what somebody was doing to them, nobody *let* themselves be done like a gift. Nobody but

Sam. He never showed off, was never saucy. He simply sank into the fuck and let Mitch watch the ride.

Adjusting his own erection, Mitch let go of Sam's cock and trailed over his balls and taint. He traced the edge of Sam's stretched hole, where Randy had three fingers plowing in and out, occasionally hooking inside.

"Mmm." Mitch sucked hard on Sam's tit, then bit the nipple until he cried out. He pressed against Randy's fingers—Randy withdrew one, inviting Mitch inside. Mitch accepted the invitation, coming in a little bit rough because he knew how much Sam liked it that way.

Sam cried out and pushed back into their hands, shivering and whimpering when the movement pulled his nipple taut in Mitch's teeth.

"There's a good slut." Randy started thrusting again, moving in counter-piston to Mitch. "Ass all full of fingers. Except you want more, don't you, Peaches. You want an ass *full*. You want everything in your ass. Because you're a sweet little slut, aren't you?"

Sam's head rolled back and landed on

Randy's shoulder. His eyes were closed in ecstasy. "Yes."

Mitch pinched hard on the right nipple while he continued to nip at the left around his words. "Gonna put more in you, Sam. Two fingers each, then three." He added the second finger and started to pump. "Tell us you want an ass full of fingers. Tell us you want us to fuck you together with our hands."

"I want you to fuck me together with your hands. *Oh.*" Sam cried out in a cascade as they each added a third finger. Sam shivered and chattered, but he rode them, bouncing his strained ass mindlessly on the clutch of digits in his butt. "*Ohgod.* I want you both to fuck me at the same time."

Mitch was down for that, but not when he was so drunk. He focused on fucking Sam as Randy sucked on his ear. They'd been so busy until Randy came they hadn't played like this, not nearly enough. "How's it feel, baby? What's it like with so much in your hole?"

"Full." Sam grunted and writhed over their tangled hands. "It's—" He jerked and let out a high-pitched sound as Randy added yet another finger.

"Kiss Mitch." Randy licked the length of Sam's neck. "Lean forward and kiss Mitch, and I'm going to use too many fingers in you for a minute, you dirty little cunt. Then I'm going to fuck you while Mitch keeps fingering you. You're gonna be so loose, honey. Loose and sore, and then we're going to spank you."

Sam nuzzled Mitch's mouth, whimpering. "And Mitch's going to marry me on Valentine's Day."

Mitch kissed Sam hard, his heart turning over at the sweet, heady combo of his fiancé being sentimental and soft as he leaned forward to be spread more lewdly than a porno shoot. When Randy replaced his fingers with his cock, riding along Mitch's three digits buried deep, Sam thrust his tongue obediently into Mitch's mouth, arching into the torture of his nipples.

"I love you," Sam whispered as Randy peeled off the condom and sprayed all over Sam's back, Mitch's fingers still working inside him.

Mitch kissed him. "I love you too."

Mitch led his lover to the spanking bench Randy had started leaving in the living room because they were using it so much. Randy put Sam in place, facing Mitch, Sam smiling as Randy drew his knees wide open. As the blows came down, Sam gave it all to Mitch, let him see, made it clear this was for him. Just like always.

Like it will be forever. And as of February fourteenth, a legally binding forever.

For the first time in months, the prospect of a wedding made Mitch smile. He tore his gaze away from Sam to watch Randy, acknowledging that Randy was, once again, a big part of that happiness.

As they did Sam together, as Randy whispered promises of making their wedding the best anybody ever had, Mitch began to plot, thinking of how he could pay Randy back for all he'd done, all he had yet to do.

RANDY EVENTUALLY DID meet Emma Day properly at New Year's. She and her fiancé hosted a party and invited Mitch and Sam, who brought Randy along. When she saw Randy, her eyes widened, but she put on a good face and welcomed him along with everyone else.

It was a nice, boring social mixer, full of people who barely knew each other and relied on wine and mixed drinks to loosen themselves up enough to have fun. Randy helped them along—he'd brought along a bottle of Jameson and Baileys, and a new deck, and after making the guests Dirty Whiskeys, he taught everyone Texas Hold 'Em. It didn't surprise him at all that Steve, Emma's fiancé, was the first one to sit down and get his hands in. He didn't know how to play, but he loved being flirted with, even by a gay man. Three drinks and five hands in, Steve had to lean on his fiancée for support.

Shortly after midnight, Randy took a break on their apartment's balcony, joining Mitch as he had a smoke. Mitch returned inside, but Randy lingered despite the cold, staring out across the sad little town and imagining the lights of Vegas from the top of a casino. When he felt someone come up behind him, he turned, grinning when he saw it was Emma.

"Hello, hostess. Nice party."

"Thanks to you." She leaned on the railing and looked out the same as Randy, though he knew she imagined different things. "I think I suck at throwing parties. It was so boring, and I didn't know how to fix it."

"Parties are all about creating a space for people. There's nothing wrong with relaxing around a campfire or on a deck. But if you want to make sure people have fun, you have to work them. Food, drink, activities. Or people. It's why drugs and alcohol are so popular at these gigs. Even if you don't have a people person on the guest list, get people smashed enough and they'll turn animals all on their own."

Emma stared at him a moment, then shook her head. "I really thought you were an asshole when I first met you, but you're not."

"I *am* an asshole. Everyone is. Some people hide it better than others, but I like to lay it out right away. Saves time."

"So did you use all your condoms?"

"Yep. They worked out better than I anticipated. I hadn't thought about how much the point of origin would matter, but that's been a *real* treat." He leaned sideways on the rail to face her. "So, let's talk wedding, honey. Sam keeps listing you as his one person he thinks will come stand up for him on his side. How true is that? Are you down for the nice parts and the naughty parts? Also, who is he overlooking, maybe at school? Though honestly, having sat in that cafeteria for a few hours, I suspect he's right. You people are a bunch of fish."

"Wait—what? Of course I'm going to Sam's wedding. I keep saying I'll help plan, but he tells me no. And yes, the naughty and nice parts, whatever that means. But what do you mean, I'm a fish?"

He patted her head. "Don't worry about the fish comment. Let's talk afterparty. How do you feel about a leather-themed reception at a gay bar?"

Emma's eyes widened. "Oh. Wow, really? You think Sam would like it? He hasn't said anything about being into something like that."

Randy smiled patiently. "Princess, I *know* Sam would like it. It's you I'm not sure about."

"What? You mean—" She blushed. "You

mean...*Sam*?"

Randy gave her a moment to catch up, then pressed on. "Is that a yes or no?" When she only continued to blush, Randy sighed. "Look—it's fine. I figured as much. But I think he wants you to stand as witness at the ceremony at least. I'm thinking of having the whole thing in Des Moines, but the ceremony will be *nice*, per Sam's request. Though it'll be on Valentine's Day. You can skip the after-party and go have your own, but it's important to him you're there for the ceremony itself. I'm willing to grease your wheels however necessary to make that happen."

"Stop." Emma held up both hands. "You're acting like I don't care about Sam. Of course I'll be there for his ceremony. And—well, tell me more about this reception. You just keep surprising me is all."

"Yeah, well, here's the deal—Sam's been sad for a long time now, and I know you're all focused on your own show, but a drunk mole could plan a straight wedding."

She had chosen an unfortunate moment to sip at her drink and nearly choked on it, spitting most of it back into her cup. "*Excuse *me.* I'll have you know planning my wedding has been *extremely stressful* and I—"

Randy shut her up with a flick of his wrist. "Save it. I know what *stress* you've been dealing with, and it's nothing on what Sam's been dealing with, which you'd know if you'd been paying half a fuck's worth of attention. All you're doing is arguing with your mother and the wedding planner and worrying about what color swatch matches the icing. *He* has got so many fucking handicaps it makes me scream. He hasn't told you how many times he's been turned away without exactly being turned away. And you aren't thinking about how much help you're getting financially where he's not getting any at all. Not to mention you have piles of family, and he has his horrid aunt and uncle, and Mitch has a father from hell and a mother who abandoned him when he was eight. They have me. And you. So shut up about who has a stressful planning session and help me figure this shit out."

She blinked at him for a second, then nodded, squaring her shoulders. "You're right. Okay. Sorry. I'm in. Tell me what we need to do. How can I help?"

"I need ideas. Help me brainstorm. Sam's a special guy, and so is Mitch, and they deserve to have something that isn't an also-ran. But this goddamn town." He gestured vaguely at Middleton and shook his head.

Emma relaxed a little. "I know what you mean. Though you're right about everything you said, it's *not* easy to plan my wedding either. There are so many *people*. And they all have ideas on how I should get married."

"Here's a tip, hon—don't ever live your life for anybody but yourself, especially not with something as significant as getting married. If you start that now, you'll never stop. You want to swallow the great suburban dream, that's one thing. You put it on because you think that's what you're supposed to do, you're in for a world of hurting." He rubbed his arms through his jacket. "I think I've had enough Iowa winter. I'm going back inside. But if you want to help me plan their wedding, holler. Who knows. You might learn a trick or two for your own."

She watched him go, and Randy smiled to himself, knowing it wouldn't be long before she gave him a call.

CHAPTER SIX

EMMA DID CALL Randy, the next day in fact. She began assisting him with his preparatory adventures, going so far as to take a day trip with him down to Des Moines to scout for a ceremony site.

"Shouldn't Sam or Mitch be along?" She braced against the dash as Randy took a corner. "God, this van sucks."

"You be nice to my ride. And no, they're just going to attend the finale. This is my present to them: sorting it out. Making it special. And a surprise."

"Got it. So what are we looking at today?"

"Venues. I've already secured the reception, plus I have several candidates for a honeymoon suite, and I have some ideas for the ceremony. But I want to see it all in person, and I want you to see it too. I know the Vegas Sam pretty well, but the Middleton edition sometimes stymies me."

Emma frowned. "There are different editions of Sam?"

"Hell yes. I know the one who rode cross-country with a guy he barely knew and cavorted all over Vegas with me and his boyfriend. The one who worries about people at Walmart judging him throws me for a loop."

"He never really told me what he did in Vegas. I don't know much about him meeting Mitch."

Randy glanced sideways at her. "Is that a request to be told?"

She considered the question for some time before replying. "I don't know. I mean—yes. I want to know. But I don't want him to be upset if I hear about it, especially if the stories don't come from him. Except I feel like ever since he came back I don't know him. It's weird because he had some big sex adventure, but he's more reserved around me than he's ever been. I don't know what to do with that."

"He had a lot more than a sex adventure. He did all kinds of things. Learned things, taught other people things, me included."

Emma sighed. "Tell me. At least show me what your Sam looks like. Not the one who sat plastered to Mitch at my party like he was being polite to be there. Because once upon a time *he* would have been the one to start games and make everyone laugh."

"Well, to start, he's who I used all the condoms on." Randy waited while Emma goggled. "Still want to hear the rest?"

"You're making that up." Emma kept shaking her head. "He's with Mitch."

"Yep. And sometimes we do him together. Sam's seriously kinky, and he loves an edge of exposure and shame. They do fine on their own, but Mitch is frank about how much more fun it is when he's sharing Sam. But then, Sam's been blowing straight guys in the bathroom since high school. You knew about that, right?"

From her expression, she clearly didn't. "I…I knew he was with a lot of guys, but in the bathroom? At *school*?"

Randy decided not to tell her about the return of Keith Jameson into Sam's sex life. "He had a thing, especially for the ones who would fuck him but then bait him publicly after."

Emma stared at the highway as if the whole world had changed color on her. "So you fuck him. With Mitch. He…watches?" She blushed scarlet. "I shouldn't be asking you this."

"Why not? The worst thing that happens is this makes Sam feel shameful, which in the end will just get him hard. I guess you could judge him, which would suck, but I'm betting on that not being your game. I think *you* would like to blow a guy in a bathroom—if you knew it was safe. You strike me as somebody with the whole *Fifty Shades* trilogy in your closet."

This time her blush was slightly different. "No. But I like a good erotic romance. I didn't like *Fifty Shades*. I thought Grey was a tool."

"What's different in the romances you *do* like?"

"The women can be sexy, sexual, love getting fucked, but the guys aren't dicks. I…I love the three-way stuff. I don't know that I want to have that. Though I'd try, maybe, with the right people. If I knew it was safe. I love the idea two guys and a girl. And—" Her blush went deep. "I like the ones best where the guys will fuck the girl and each other too."

Randy snorted. "Shit, honey. You should have me over and let me get you and your boyfriend drunk. We could have a party."

"Wait—you're bi?"

Emma got the same look that Sam did when he was approaching a forbidden delight, and it turned Randy the hell on. "Nope. Not even close. But that doesn't mean I can't drive the bus, princess. That's my kink: head-fucking. It would be all kinds of fun, getting you and your straight-laced fiancé to cut loose with me."

"I…don't think so." She said the words, but Randy could see them taking root, and they made him smile.

"Standing offer. You give me the come-hither, and I'll seduce you and your boy together."

"He'd never go for it."

"I bet you—and bear in mind, I never lose a bet—he would go for it in a hot minute, if he thought you wanted it. Test it out. Next time you're in bed, say, 'Randy said the craziest thing to me.' Then make it clear you love the idea. Though…he'd want your vag off-limits for penetration. Which is fine."

Emma touched her hair, flustered, but definitely thinking about three-ways. "So you fuck Sam?"

"Every day I'm with him. Well, if Mitch is out of town, he gets funny about it, but I almost enjoy that more, having to wear him down."

"Did you fuck him today?"

"Nope. He had to get up too early. But last night we played his favorite game: watch TV."

Emma laughed, a beautiful mixture of nerves and wickedness. "Okay, I'll bite. What's *watch TV*?"

"Remember that Sam's kink is the shame and exposure. He likes being turned into an object. Which gets rough when he knows how much you love him, and vetting strangers is always tough. So we play watch TV. Diddle him while watching a show. Last night it was that he had to give one of us a blowjob while the other fingered him and slapped his butt."

"Does he want you telling me all this?"

"Oh hell no. But I don't think that's a good thing. You're supposed to be the best friend. You don't have to know all the kinky deets, but him being kinky should at least be something you're okay with."

"I'm totally okay with it." She sighed. "Fuck, I'm jealous."

Randy grinned. "You want to hear more? Because I've got all kinds of stories."

God, she was *cute* when she blushed. Randy hoped to hell she let her man see this side of her. "I want to hear the rest of watch TV."

"That's pretty much it. We put on something boring and talk about the show while we play with his body. Like he's nothing more than a remote. Last night he started with Mitch's cock, and Mitch didn't say a word to him except to direct him. I had him spread his knees so I could really get in there, make him squirm, and every time I did, he'd wiggle, and I'd slap his butt. He *loves* being spanked. Makes all kinds of great noises."

Emma was flushed in a very different way now. "Jesus. You shouldn't tell me this."

Randy laughed. "God, you two are the

same. You love it. I'd tell you to frig one out, but you'd probably self-combust from that much shame."

She went red as a tomato. "I'm not going to masturbate in front of you!"

"You could, though. You're not quite there, but you could. With your man, probably. You *want* to, that's the thing—which is the same as Sam." He tapped the steering wheel. "Maybe that's the way to play this. Maybe we should all hang out drunk, and you make me tell you stories about him."

"You really are crazy, you know that?" Emma eyed him speculatively. "So are you their other boyfriend or something? Do you have a Mitch of your own?"

"I don't want a Mitch, and no, I'm not a boyfriend. I'm a friend you can fuck."

"So you're nobody's boyfriend?"

"Please. Do I seem like I could be?"

Emma looked thoughtful. "It would take somebody pretty singular."

Randy snorted. "It'd take a fucking miracle."

They rode in silence for some time after that, and when they began chatting again, they stayed on benign topics such as weather and music until they pulled into the western suburbs of the city.

"What are you thinking for the ceremony?" Emma asked.

"I'm down to a bed and breakfast, a wedding chapel, and…that's it really. There are a million sites I'd love to consider outdoors, but Sam and Mitch want Valentine's Day, and they don't have a lot of money, and neither do I, so I'm a little boxed in. Not to mention almost everything is taken—this is the only B&B with a vacancy, and they're holding it for me with someone on the waiting list ready to pop if I don't. I have one Hail Mary I'm saving in case of complete failure." He aimed the van toward an exit. "B&B first."

The bed and breakfast was cute enough, and the people were nice, but Randy wasn't feeling it. He wasn't quite sure why until Emma pointed it out.

"If you use this, they'll expect Sam and Mitch to stay here, and given what you're saying about how the wedding night will go down, this might be the wrong kind of intimate." She wrinkled her nose. "Besides, everything smells like perfume."

Randy nodded with a grimace. "All right. Let's hope this wedding chapel is better, then."

Unfortunately, it wasn't. The proprietors were wonderful, charming, beautiful people. The space was the right size, and while there were several weddings booked that day, the chapel had plenty of other openings. The problem was the room didn't feel right to Randy at all. Technically it gave Sam everything he wanted, but it was dark, cramped, and felt like a Vegas chapel's sad, neglected cousin. He'd worried about that from the pictures online, but the real thing was even more disappointing and depressing.

"What now?" Emma asked as they got back into the van. "Your Hail Mary?"

"I guess. The good news is that it's just a few blocks from the reception. The shit news is that it's outside."

"Well, are you going to tell me where it is, or what?"

"Nope. I'm going to show you."

Randy drove into the downtown, navigating the one-way streets with a lot of swearing until he had them driving up Locust, heading for the west side of the capitol building. He gestured at the golden dome glittering in the muted winter sun. "There. That's my Hail Mary."

Emma looked around, confused—then up. "Oh—*oh*. Randy, that's a *brilliant* idea. The Iowa State Capitol. How fitting is that—the whole reason they can get married."

"No, technically that would be the Iowa Supreme Court, but it's not as pretty."

"Can you have a ceremony here?"

"Totally, and better yet, it's free. It doesn't have to be reserved—which means it's not exclusive, but I doubt there will be a rush. Only outside, though, so it'll be cold. It could be really fucking cold. But it doesn't cost a dime, and it comes self-themed."

"I think this is perfect. Screw the cold. They can wear winter coats and have hand warmers. Like Mitch was going to wear a suit anyway."

"Oh, he's wearing a suit." Randy pulled the van into a parking spot and stared at the capitol building, imagining the wedding happening there. "So it'll be them, you, me, and whoever we can bring over from the bar. You know, maybe this is perfect in a lot of ways. And who knows, we could get lucky, and it'll be sixty that day. This is the Midwest in winter after all. Anything from thirty below to seventy above is fair play. Shit odds, though. But it doesn't take long to say a few fancy words and *I do*, *me too*, I guess."

"It'll be you, me, and Steve, by the way. When you book the honeymoon suite, I'm getting the two of us a room in the same place."

"Good." Randy tapped his thumb on the steering wheel. "What about Sam's aunt and uncle? Should I just write them off?"

"You have to invite them to the ceremony. And…honestly, I don't think it's a given they won't come. Unlikely, but…well, let's say in the past year I've learned a lot about Sam's aunt."

"Don't tell me she has hidden depths."

"No. But under all the barbs and judgment is Sam's mom's sister."

Randy said nothing, only nodded, but he made a mental note to deliver that invite in person. He'd also ensure if Delia did come, she didn't rain on Sam and Mitch's big day.

Emma turned in her seat. "So where is the reception? What bar are you talking about? Because you have me all curious about this."

Randy grinned. "I'll show you. But don't tell Sam and Mitch. It's my favorite surprise."

As JANUARY ROLLED on, Randy's wedding preparations got more and more intense. He teased Sam and Mitch relentlessly about how much they were going to love it, but outside of a trip to Ames to get fitted for their suits, he kept even the smallest details to himself. He began to disappear more and more often, sometimes for days at a time. Sam tried to get information out of Emma, who had been working with him, but Emma would only grin mischievously and promise it was going to be awesome.

Mitch was sure it would be. It was strange to be so removed from their wedding, but mostly he liked how happy Sam had become again. The light was back in Sunshine's eyes, a spring in his step. When they made love, he was soft and sweet, and when they fucked dirty and played, he let go more completely, the release a celebration, not a coping mechanism.

This was all because of Randy, Mitch knew. And as the wedding drew closer, Mitch decided it was time he did something about it.

One weekend when Randy was off on another planning mission, Mitch took Sam on a jaunt to Minneapolis. He had a job, so they went in Old Blue, but in Mitch's mind the greater task was having a conversation he'd been trying to work out for weeks.

"It's nice to get away." As they navigated onto the highway, heading north, Sam stared out across the wintry landscape. "I feel like all I'm doing lately is going to school and working." He laughed softly. "Since Randy showed up, I guess also having kinky sex."

That was a good segue, Mitch decided. "I wanted to talk to you about that. About Randy." He shifted his grip on the wheel. "I don't think we could have done this without him. Not just the wedding, but everything. It's been nice having him here."

"Yeah." Sam turned in his seat, and when Mitch glanced his way, he saw his lover smiling a slow, sweet smile. "I wish he could live with us. But probably that would get weird, eventually."

"He couldn't ever live here long-term. I can't believe how long he's put up with this winter." Though, honestly, Mitch wasn't surprised. Randy would do anything for his friends.

"Fun as it is to be with him, the three of us…sometimes I think it makes him sad." Sam tucked his feet beneath him on the seat. "I think he wishes he had somebody too. Somebody his alone."

That, Mitch couldn't give Randy, unfortunately. "I thought we should find a way to thank him for everything. Something at the wedding. Or rather, something after the wedding."

"What do you mean?"

Why did this make Mitch so nervous? He fumbled for his Winstons. After a long drag, he made himself spit his thoughts out. "Well, I wondered if maybe you in particular should say thanks. That night." His stomach knotted. "Unless you don't want to."

Sam was quiet too long, and Mitch sucked

the cigarette down way too fast. But when Sam finally spoke, he wasn't mad. "Do you mean you'd be okay with me fucking him on our wedding night? Really?"

Mitch couldn't quite trust he hadn't fucked this up. "Only if it was okay with you. But…yeah. I think it would be…good."

"I guess that surprises me is all. It's kind of a big day."

Shit, did Sam think Mitch didn't consider their wedding special? God, he'd stepped in it. "We can forget it. You're right. It was a dumb idea."

"I never said it was a dumb idea."

Mitch glanced his way, then did a double take as he realized Sam was turned on. "So…you'd be okay with it?"

"Okay? God. I'm hot right now simply thinking about it." Sam adjusted himself in his jeans, but it didn't seem to relieve him much. "You'd seriously let him fuck me. In front of you. On *our wedding night*. God, that's so dirty."

Mitch put his spent end into the butt bucket and reached for a new one. "Actually, I thought he should do you first alone. On the bed where we'd sleep that night. Let him have you for an hour all on his own. We could play together after, but first, the two of you."

Sam swallowed hard. Even in the dim light Mitch could see how turned on Sam was. "We don't usually play like that. Not if you're around. Not often even when you're not."

"Right. We won't tell him in advance—but that night, you will. You'll go right up to him and tell him he gets you all by himself. You suggest it." Sam bit his lip and shut his eyes, touching himself, and Mitch grinned. "In fact, beg him to fuck you. I'll listen outside the room. Or sit at the bar downstairs, or whatever. It'll only be the two of you, though. And you have to do whatever he says."

"Kissing too?"

Mitch hesitated, walls going up as emotions churned inside him. "Everything but that."

Sam clutched his erection through his jeans. "Mitch—fuck."

Mitch smiled and exhaled a ribbon of smoke as he saw a sign for a rest stop a few miles ahead. "I think that's a good present for both of you. Make you whore yourself out to my best friend on your wedding night. You can tell him I ordered you to do it, to throw yourself at him—in fact, probably you should. It'll turn you both on. Just make sure he fucks you hard. I want to know he's been there when I have you."

Sam arched his back against the seat. "Please, please tell me to jerk myself off."

"Nope." Mitch slowed down, not quite ready to let Sam have his release. "Sit there and squirm and practice how you're going to beg him. What are you going to ask him to do to you?"

Sam whimpered, but Mitch made him describe it all, every filthy detail. Sometimes Mitch offered suggestions, which only made Sam wilder. By the time he pulled off into the rest stop, Sam was incoherent. When Mitch told him to get out of his seat and strip, Sam clambered out of his seat and tugged off his clothes in less than twenty seconds flat.

They found a parking spot in the back of the rest stop, and Sam climbed naked onto Mitch's lap. But when Mitch reached for the lube on the dash, Sam shook his head and pushed Mitch's hand to his ass, where a greased-up plug quickly came away, revealing Sam stretched and ready.

"I figured you'd want to fuck me on the way." Sam kissed Mitch as he undid his belt buckle. "I wanted you to be able to go right in." He bit Mitch's lip. "Please, go right in. Fuck me hard. Fuck me really, really hard."

Mitch freed his cock and drove straight inside, taking in Sam's body as he arched and cried out in a mixture of pain and pleasure, running a hand down his torso. "Since it makes you so hot when I give you away, maybe I should put out a call on Grindr in the Cities. Let them know I have a slutty boy who'll be in town for the night and gets hot when I make him whore for strangers."

"Whatever you want." Sam's eyes rolled back in his head as he bounced himself up and down on Mitch's cock. "I'll do whatever you want. I love you, Mitch. So much."

I love you too, Mitch thought, but couldn't say out loud because Sam had plastered their mouths together again. Taking Sam's hips tight in his hands, Mitch sucked hard on Sam's tongue, mashed his cock between their thrusting bodies, and drove them both home.

CHAPTER SEVEN

A WEEK BEFORE the wedding, Randy went to Cherry Hill.

It had snowed three days ago, but now it was fifty and sunny, and Randy had been in Iowa long enough to find that nearly tropical. As he parked his van on the street in front of Delia and Norman's house, he squinted at the sun and glanced around, imagining Sam living in the crispy-pressed, high-sterilization that was his aunt and uncle's housing development. Simply standing there made Randy feel depressed. He couldn't imagine coming home there every single day.

He couldn't imagine having to call this *home*.

As Randy ambled up Delia's sidewalk, he could feel the eyes of the neighbors on him, metaphorically if not literally. He knew without looking Delia would be at her window, trying to work out who it was coming to her front door. Randy hadn't made any extra effort to clean himself up, so he imagined she was freaking out over the grubby, jean-jacket guy in motorcycle boots heading up to her house.

Good. In his opinion, Delia Biehl could do with a little squirming.

He almost laughed out loud when she answered the door without opening the storm door that separated them. If his mission wasn't so important, he would have fucked with her, tried to live up to her fantasies of a dangerous stranger. But he had a job to do, so he smiled his least-alligator smile and held out the wedding invitation. "Delia. I'm Randy, Sam's friend who's planning his wedding. You keep not replying to the invitations I'm sending, so I thought I'd bring one to your house so you could tell me yes or no to my face."

He liked the way that made her sputter. Poor thing didn't get many blunt speakers, did she? "I—" She opened and closed her mouth several times, but she couldn't seem to speak.

Randy braced a hand against the doorframe, leaving space for her to open the door if she chose. "I know you aren't Sam's biggest fan, but I am. He doesn't have a lot of family, but I know he'd want me to reach out to you. Emma also thinks I should. Me, I wanted to skip it because I figured you'd do this, pull passive-aggressive shit where you string everybody out. I hate to tell you, it didn't work. I'm the only one who knows you haven't sent a reply. So you're going to tell me, right now, if you're coming or not. And if you are coming, I'm letting you know here and now if you try to sour Sam and Mitch's special day, I will visit ruin on your head like you don't even know to dream of."

Delia gasped and drew back, pulling her best *well, I never* face, but she still didn't know how to respond to Randy, how to behave around him at all. She simply stood staring at him. She wasn't quite stripped bare, but she was undone and vulnerable.

"I don't know who you think you are or why you think you have a right to threaten to assault me in my own home, sir."

"No one is threatening to assault anyone. Listen carefully to what I'm saying, *Mrs. Biehl.*" Randy stretched his smile to dangerous lengths. "I'm saying, if you come to their wedding and make them miserable with catty comments and ill-timed remarks, I will return the favor. You're an active, social person in this town. It wouldn't take me a day to make you *achingly* sorry you spoke out of turn."

Delia's mouth fell open, and she clutched at her pearls—yes, she really was wearing a string of them.

Randy went in for the kill.

"I know you." He leaned closer to the storm door, speaking softly enough that she had to strain, but loud enough to get through the glass. "I know who you are, Delia, and I understand. When Sam first told me about you, I thought you were a cartoon, because he made you out to be such a bitch it was hard to believe, but then I saw you at the store, around town, and I got it."

He jerked his head at the fireplace mantel behind Delia, at the funeral urn sitting there—the one Randy knew was empty because Sam had stolen his mother's ashes.

"She was the pretty one, wasn't she? Sharyle was smart and pretty and bubbly, like Sam, and everybody liked her. Even when she got knocked up, everybody liked her. Even when she got sick and died, everyone liked her—and then she was gone, and she was a saint. You loved her because she was your sister, but you hated her too, hated how she got what you always wanted. She was dying, and you had a husband and a fancy house, but you still wished you could be her. And then she did you one worse—she had a son when you couldn't. A sweet, wonderful boy who everybody loved as much as his mom. Who couldn't love you."

Delia blinked at him, tears in her eyes. "How—?"

Randy waved a hand. "Easy. Nobody hates like you do without a reason. And why else would you be such a bitch? Except that's where you fucked up, sweetie. Because Sam's amazing. You had him that whole time—no, he'd never have been your biological son, but he could have been close. You wouldn't have had an empty, lonely Christmas this year or any other year. You'd have had Sam and his boyfriend. You could have been helping him plan. Instead of me befriending strangers so he can have a crowd, you could have provided the real deal. You could be filling a church with your friends who would give him gift cards and twenties and make him feel included and wanted. Which was all *you* ever wanted, ironically enough. Except you never figured out that the way to feel included yourself was to be that for other people."

He held up the invitation, pressing it against the screen between them. "Here's your last chance. Come to his wedding. Be his family. Send him into the next part of his life with a smile. Just know if you decline, this is it. He won't come to you again. And with Sam, there might be grandchildren one day. There might be a lot of amazing things. You come to his wedding, he'll remember. You don't, he'll remember that too." Randy waited, letting that sink in. "So what'll it be, Delia? Yes, or no?"

She stared at him a long time, full of hatred and misery and sadness. "No," she said at last, and slammed her front door in his face.

Randy pulled the invitation off the screen,

tucked it into his pocket. "That's what I thought," he said, and ambled back down the sidewalk to his van.

FOUR DAYS BEFORE the wedding, Sam and Mitch sat on the couch watching TV when a knock sounded on their apartment door. Since Randy was off playing poker and laying schemes, Sam went to answer. When Sam gasped in surprise and said, "Delia," Mitch got up and went to stand with his husband-to-be.

Usually when Delia showed up at their apartment she was angry about something, but this time she seemed beaten up. Her eyes were red, as if she'd been crying, and she held a ceramic urn in her hands. "She's gone. I—I don't know how, Sam, but she's gone."

Mitch was about to ask who was gone, but something in Sam's expression made him pause.

"Come on in." Sam stepped back to let his aunt inside. "Why don't you come sit down?"

Delia went to the kitchen, where she put the urn on the counter and lifted the lid, tipping it to show Sam. "Nothing. I lifted it, and it was so light, so I opened it, and it was almost empty. I—I don't know what happened, Sam. I'm so sorry."

Sam put a hand on hers, but even as he comforted her, he appeared battle-ready. "She's gone because I took her, Delia. When I went off with Mitch, I took her with me."

Ashes, Mitch realized. Sam's mother's ashes. Apparently Delia never knew Sam had them.

Shit.

Delia blinked at Sam, over and over. "You…took her? The ashes? Out of the urn? On a…*road trip*?" She said the word *road trip* like most people would say *sex-fueled orgy*.

Not far off the mark, really. Though it had been more than that. So much more than that. Especially for those ashes.

"Yes, I took her with me." Sam folded his hands in front of himself, patient but firm. "She would have hated that urn. She would have loved a road trip. I sprinkled her ashes all over the western United States. She's still on Mitch's dash, and now she's been all over the continent. To Mexico. To Canada. She's been more places than I have. That seemed a lot better end for her than sitting in an ugly urn on your shelf."

Mitch got ready for a fight, but to his surprise, Delia deflated. After fishing a tissue out of her purse, she dabbed at her eyes. "I was going to give you the urn. As a wedding present."

Sam softened, but not much. "That was nice of you. Except she wasn't ever yours to give. She was my mom."

Now Delia's eyes lit with anger. "She was *my* sister."

"Yeah. And you loved her about as much as you love me. Which is to say, not at all."

Delia turned to stare out the kitchen window. They stood there awkwardly, nobody sure what to do next. Then Delia spoke.

"When Sharyle was pregnant with you, I was pregnant too."

Sam blinked. "But you weren't even married to Uncle Norman yet."

Delia kept wiping her eyes. "We got engaged because I was pregnant. Neither one of us was ready, but after watching Sharyle go through everything with no husband or boyfriend at all, Norm felt he should do the right thing. We didn't really love each other, but we decided that would come with time. So we announced our engagement and made plans. We set it up so we'd have the wedding before I'd show, but not so soon it appeared that's what it was. We planned to tell people after the ceremony, quietly—people would figure it out, but at least we could have a nice wedding first, without a scandal." She swallowed hard and shut her eyes. "Three weeks before our wedding day I miscarried."

Mitch's breath caught in his chest. He watched Delia's shoulders shake, saw her sorrow, and for the first time in his life, he felt pity for Sam's aunt.

Sam looked like he wanted to go to her but didn't dare. "Delia," he said, but that was all he could manage.

A bottle uncorked, she kept going. "We never told anyone about it, so no one knew. Sharyle did, but I couldn't stand to see her because she was almost ready to give birth to you, and now I was empty. Empty for good—I couldn't have any more children, they said. So now I was getting married, barren, to a man I didn't love and who didn't love me. We thought about calling it off, but we were both too scared of what people would say. So we got married. Meanwhile, Sharyle had you out of wedlock with no support and developed MS, and then cancer, and yet I envied her every single day." She bit her lip, let out a short sob, and shook her head. "I didn't want to hate you. But I couldn't love you. It hurt too much."

Sam went up behind her, shut his eyes, and hugged her.

She wept silently, brushing his hands as they closed over her arms, as if she didn't dare touch him. "I can't come to your wedding," she whispered. "I'm sorry. I just can't."

Sam patted her forearm. "It's okay."

She shook her head. "It's not. But I still can't." She extricated herself, shaking, from his embrace. "I'll take the urn back, because it still reminds me of her. But I'll send you a check. And I'll think of you on your big day."

"Thank you." Mitch took Sam's hand in his.

She hugged Sam awkwardly and touched Mitch's arm. Then she scooped up the urn, and she left.

They stood in the kitchen, staring at the door where she'd disappeared.

"Wow," Sam said at last.

Mitch kissed his hair and led him back to the couch. "Let's finish our show."

They sat back down together, holding each other close. Though while they both stared at the television, Mitch knew neither one of them could think about anything but Delia Biehl and her sad, lonely story.

It wasn't something Mitch or anybody else could fix, that sorrow. But it was something he'd never forget.

CHAPTER EIGHT

Valentine's Day—Mitch and Sam's wedding day—dawned bright, cool, and free of precipitation. Mitch had worried they would have bad weather, as they'd been saying there could be a blizzard just a few days before. Randy had admitted the wedding was out of town and had explained to them in no uncertain terms that if there *was* a blizzard, they were going to Des Moines ahead of it and camping out. The storm tracked north, however, and in fact temperatures were due to hit the forties by the afternoon. Which seemed to relieve Randy. When Mitch asked why, Randy told him. And Mitch about fell over.

"We're getting married *outside*? In *February*?"

Randy shrugged, but his expression made

it plain this hadn't been his initial plan. "It'll work out, I promise. And you'll love it. Sam especially."

That was all he'd give them, refusing to say anything about the wedding, making them a brunch neither Sam nor Mitch was hungry for. When Randy got tired of their fidgeting, he kicked their asses at poker until, at one, Randy glanced at the clock and slapped Mitch on the ass.

"Go get into your monkey suit. We've got a drive ahead of us."

Everyone wore a suit, Randy included—dark gray, because Randy said black washed Mitch out too much. The suits, all three of them, were the only thing Mitch had paid for, because Randy wouldn't let him touch anything else.

Sam came out of the bedroom with his bow tie dangling from his collar. He looked wickedly delicious, though he also appeared to be frustrated. "Can't we get dressed once we get down there?"

"No. We're heading directly to the ceremony." Randy took over the tie, his own already knotted expertly at his throat. "And don't try to tell me your suit is uncomfortable. It's tailored to fit you perfectly, and it's quality wool."

He had to help Mitch with his tie too—even if Mitch had known how to do the tie, he was pretty sure his fingers wouldn't have worked. He was *getting married.* In a matter of hours. Somewhere in Des Moines.

Holy shit. *Holy fucking shit.*

Sam seemed to be having much the same revelation, and once again, they couldn't have functioned without Randy. He ushered them through packing overnight bags, then gave up and finished it himself as Sam and Mitch stared stupidly at each other in the kitchen. He drove, taking them in his van, though he surprised them by swinging over to pick up Emma and Steve, who also had an overnight bag and were dressed in their wedding finery. Emma wore a red velvet gown that looked like elegant sin beneath a beautiful faux-fur wrap, and Steve had a gray suit that matched everyone else's.

Having them along was a coup because Emma and Randy flirted, Randy and Steve flirted, Emma and Sam flirted, and eventually they got Mitch to loosen up to wisecrack a bit too. Mostly, though, he sat stunned by the knowledge that he was riding to his wedding.

It wasn't that he was having second thoughts, not at all—it was that never in his wildest dreams had he imagined, ever, that this would happen. When he'd been able to pretend he was straight, he hadn't thought of marrying anyone, and as soon as he admitted he was queer, he gave up all hope. When he'd grown up, that wasn't something anybody so much as wished for. Even when things like marriage equality started to be whispered, Mitch knew he wasn't the kind of guy another guy would want to settle down with.

Except he was. He was the guy Sam wanted to marry. The guy Sam *would* marry. Today.

By the time they pulled into Des Moines, Mitch was so overwhelmed he felt dizzy. Sam took his hand, kissed it, left his captain's chair to climb on Mitch's lap, and whispered encouragements in his ear. Mitch shut his eyes and clung to Sam, letting his sweet voice chase away the last of his shadows.

He *was* good enough. He *was* an all right

guy. He *could* have a happily ever after.

So long as it was with Sam Keller.

The van stopped, and Randy killed the engine. "We're here. Emma texted the guys, so they should be along shortly. Oh look. There's Kyl now."

Sam shifted on Mitch's lap and turned toward the front of the vehicle. "Randy, where are we getting married?"

"Here." Randy pointed through the dash. "Right here."

Mitch leaned over, followed Randy's gesture, and his heart seized in his chest as he gazed at the Iowa State Capitol.

He'd seen it before, the outside many times as he'd driven through Des Moines, the inside once with Sam when they'd gone to a rally at the statehouse when the legislature had threatened to take away marriage equality. Sam had been full of facts and stories about the building and the state of Iowa in general. How the dome was real gold. How Iowa had allowed interracial marriage before the Civil War and graduated the first female lawyer in the United States. Sam was proud of his home state, *very* proud.

Of course Randy had known about that.

Except right now Sam wasn't looking proud. He was whey-faced and trembling, his hand over his mouth.

Randy touched Sam's arm. "Peaches, you okay? Did I do okay? Was this bad?"

Sam nodded, accepted a tissue from Emma, and began to cry.

Randy opened his mouth, and Mitch could see the *I'm sorry* forming, but he shook his head and held up a hand. Then he put his palm on Sam's back, rubbing it soothingly, kissing his shoulder as he explained. "When he was little, Sam would come to Des Moines with his mom for her doctor's appointments, and they would stop and have picnics here, because Sam called the capitol building his palace." He slid his hand up to Sam's neck, teasing the back of his hair. "He told her he'd live there someday and have big parties outside, and she could come too."

Sam cried harder, then took hold of Randy's face and kissed him firmly on the mouth. "Thank you," he whispered, then kissed Randy again, once on each cheek.

"You're welcome," Randy whispered

back, and when he pulled away, his eyes were pretty damp.

Heart swelling as he watched the scene, Mitch thought of his plans for later in the evening and knew he'd made the right decision.

They got out of the van and headed up the steps to what in the summer was a floral dais but right now was a concrete oasis surrounded by drifts of slightly dirty snow. The steps had been cleared, and they walked up them together to the small patio area where a cluster of men and women Mitch didn't know stood.

Randy waved and greeted everyone warmly, hugging them and kissing the ladies on the cheek. He took Mitch and Sam by the arm and introduced them around—Mary, Jess, Jo, Kyl, Liam, and Mark, who had apparently been helping him set up the reception and had come now just to see the show. Two of them had official functions: Jo was taking photos, and Kyl would be their officiant. Everyone smiled and told Mitch and Sam congratulations.

"We've been helping Randy plan for

months," Liam explained, putting his arm around Mark. "We couldn't miss the main event."

"Everything's set up at the Saddle," Mark told Randy. "If it had been warmer, I think more people would have come over to watch."

"Thanks." Randy glanced around. "Okay. Sam and Mitch, you're going to ditch your coats and gloves, because the pictures won't be as nice with your clunky parkas. But this won't take long, so you can suffer through a few shivers. Jo, you set to play photographer?"

Both Jo and Mary had long blonde hair—Jo was the younger one, wearing a red knit beret and a rainbow-colored scarf. She held up a professional-grade camera. "Locked and loaded."

Mary stepped forward, extending her arms. "I'll hold your coats."

"You can't take them all," Jess said, taking point beside her. "Here, let me take them for you. Liam, you help.".

And then Sam and Mitch's wedding happened.

Randy and Emma walked up the stairs

together, looking like they were heading to an Oscar gala, not a gay wedding on the west terrace of the state capitol, and Sam and Mitch followed after. They stood holding hands before Kyl, a charming bear of a man who spoke politely but had a mischievous glint in his eye, especially when he smiled. Randy stood beside Mitch, and Emma stood beside Sam.

No one held flowers, but Emma carried the pretty glass chest Sam had bought in Arizona that held the last of his mother's ashes.

Kyl said a few words, not that Mitch had brain enough to hear them. They were variants on the standard *we are gathered here today*, tailored though to Sam and Mitch, talking about how they started with one adventure and now embarked on another, a life promised together, forever.

"And now for the vows," Kyl said.

Hand shaking, Mitch withdrew the notecard from his pocket and began to read, doing his best to occasionally meet Sam's gaze.

"I never thought I would meet someone like you, Sam." He let out a shaking breath, almost dropping the card from nerves. "I never thought I'd get married, never thought I'd have a real family. But then I met you, and you made me believe. You made me believe in all kinds of things I didn't think were possible. Love. Partners. Happily ever after." He squeezed Sam's hand, emotion burning in his chest as he took the ring Randy passed him and slipped it onto Sam's finger. "I love you, Sam Keller. I promise to love you until I die, to do everything I can to make you happy. If I can give it to you, I will. Because being with you, seeing you smile, makes me happier than I ever knew I could be."

Sam kept hold of Mitch's hand, kissed it, then withdrew a card of his own.

"Mitch, before I met you, my life seemed so dull and hopeless. But one week with you changed everything. You helped me see the world in a new way. You helped me see *myself* in a new way. You made me fall in love with you harder than I ever thought I could love anyone—and I had some seriously romantic ideas before I got started." He glanced at Emma, who produced his ring, which he slipped onto Mitch's finger. "You call me

Sunshine, but you're my star, Mitch Tedsoe. I love you, and I always will, forever and ever." He lowered his card and smiled at Mitch like a sun. "It's going to be easy to make me happy, because all I need to feel that way is to be with you."

Kyl placed his bare hands over the top of their joined ones. "By the power vested in me, I now pronounce you Sam and Mitch Keller-Tedsoe." He gave their wrists a squeeze and winked as he withdrew. "Congratulations."

Everyone cheered and clapped as Mitch and Sam went into each other's arms and sealed their marriage with a kiss.

Married. I'm married. To Sam. The thought rang in Mitch's head as he posed for photos and accepted hugs and kisses from total strangers who made it clear they were about to become some of his closest friends in Iowa.

It had actually happened. He'd asked Sam to marry him, Sam had said yes, *and now they were married.*

Legally. *Real.* It was real. Completely, totally real. Forever.

When it was Randy's turn to embrace

him, Mitch held his best friend tight, clutching at the back of his suit jacket and burying his face in Randy's neck as he tried to collect himself enough to speak. He couldn't manage it, though, and eventually Randy took pity on him and kissed his ear.

"You're fine, you goofy Old Man. You're just fine."

Mitch exhaled on a shuddering breath. "Thank you. Thank you for this. For everything."

"You haven't even seen the reception yet. Down the street at a place called the Blazing Saddle. We have the whole back half of the bar. And as it happens, it's leather night."

Mitch laughed and squeezed Randy again before letting him go. He took his coat back from Mary, who gave him a hug and a kiss, then went to claim his husband's arm so they could go to their party.

THE BLAZING SADDLE, Randy learned in his preparations for the reception, had been in the East Village of Des Moines for thirty years, weathering cultural and economic seismic shifts with a loyal, friendly clientele and its motto of *always a double, never a cover*. In his visits to the small but charming gay bar, Randy had met businessmen and blue collars, old queens and sassy young things. From what Randy could gather, gay clubs came and went all around them, but the Saddle was the Iowa original, steadfast and unwavering. The pride parade passed down its street, and the burgeoning Saturday night party and Sunday festival happened right outside its front doors.

As Randy ushered Sam and Mitch through those doors on Valentine's Day evening, the entire bar let out a cheer, raising their glasses in toast and tossing confetti. Jo made them pause for a few photos—Mary had the cake ready, which Sam and Mitch sliced together before performing the traditional circus of stuffing it in each other's faces. Once that act was completed and photographed for posterity, the rest of the cake was passed to the small but enthusiastic crowd. Randy led Sam and Mitch to the front part of the bar, letting Jo get plenty of pictures of them milling around. He gave the bartender a word, and Kylie's "All I See" played over the sound system. Everyone cheered as Sam and Mitch had their first dance together on the small stage by the front window.

Then, with all the niceties seen to and standard photo ops achieved, Randy led the wedding party into the back room, where Liam, Mark, and Kyl waited with the accouterments for the next stage of the game.

"Time to change," Randy told them, as the door shut and he began to strip out of his suit. He nodded at Liam, who held out a garment bag to Mitch. "Levi's and leather for you. Mark brought along an assortment of accessories. I'll let you decide if you go harness or vest. *You,* however." Randy pointed at Sam. "Go with Liam, who has something special set up on the stage."

"Stage?" Sam echoed, but Liam only smiled and took his hand, leading Sam away.

"You're going to love it. God, I wish *I* could wear it. But I'm wearing my puppy outfit, and wings just don't work with my gear."

"*Wings?*" Sam glanced over his shoulder at Randy, wide-eyed, but Randy only grinned.

Randy put on his leather pants and vest, knowing he'd have to peel them off with a crowbar by the time the night was over, but not really caring because he was pretty sure Mitch and Sam were only having a leather wedding reception just the once. The girls took turns commandeering the bathrooms to get into their costumes—Jo wore a fetching corset, Jess a gorgeous tit-centric leather gown. Mary declined to change, focusing instead on helping Emma into the outfit Jo had picked out for her: a gorgeous black sheath with studded collar and long leather gloves. Jo gave her a flogger too, which was a bit of a mixed message with the collar, but from the way Steve—in jeans and a leather vest—stilled as she practiced a swing under Jo's careful tutelage, Randy thought it would probably work out okay.

Mitch chose a vest and chaps, then went out front to have a cigarette with Mark while Liam continued to transform Sam behind the partition on the stage. Randy, in his leather gear, leaned against the wall and grinned as he listened to Sam's squeals and Liam's gentle cajoling. Eventually he surmised from the absence of protestations and whispers that Sam was trussed, though he stayed behind as Liam got into his pup clothes.

"Okay, we're ready," Liam called at last, and came out wearing a harness, tight pants, and paws but holding his hood as he led Sam into view.

Everyone oohed and ahhed and complimented Sam, who was, no question, the sexiest, cutest cupid anybody ever did see. He wore white leather boy shorts that showed plenty of ass and lots of crotch through the groin lacing. Liam had applied eyeliner around Sam's eyes too, making him seem like a deliciously tripped-out angel. The wings were fantastic, snow white and full of real feathers. Randy had loved them when they'd arrived in the mail, but he *adored* them on Peaches.

Grinning, Randy went to the base of the stage and held out his hand. "Hey, married man. Ready to go have a party?"

Smiling a little shyly, Sam took his hand. "Yeah."

It was fun to watch Sam and Mitch encounter each other in their gear—Sam looked like he wanted to blow Mitch right there, and Mitch, as Randy knew he would, stared at his husband as if he finally appeared on the outside the way he Mitch thought of him inside and out. Debauched angel, an invitation in his gaze and a light in his heart.

Yep. It was going be a *fantastic* party.

And it was. Randy led their leather party into the main room—not everyone was in gear, as it was still early, but a lot of people were, and everyone present appreciated the scenery. Sam and Mitch did a tour of the room, escorted and introduced by Liam and Kyl. Meanwhile, Jo and Mark helped Randy arrange the sound system in the back room and got everything set up for the dance and karaoke party. When everything was ready, they lured the guests over to cut loose in honor of Sam and Mitch.

At the start of the night, Sam and Mitch only knew Randy, Emma, and Steve, but by the end of the evening they had one hundred and fifty new friends. Drag kings and queens, leather daddies who sang show tunes, old timers and newbs who happened to drop in to see the show—everyone had a great time, making Sam and Mitch's wedding reception the best party anyone could have. Food appeared on silver trays around ten, bite-sized nibbles Kyl had made himself. Jess passed around a leather cap several times, collecting offerings for the groom and groom. Some people had come prepared, bearing gift cards and presents they left at the bar, but most simply passed over cash—and plenty of condoms. There were also, Randy noticed, several phone numbers.

They danced, all of them—Randy and Sam, Randy and Mitch, Sam and Mitch, Randy and Liam, Sam and Jo—at some point everyone paired up with everyone, for dirty grinds and silly sways, whatever they felt like, however they wanted it. Liam and Sam in particular made a beautifully slutty team, and Jo got plenty of pictures. As Sam got a few drinks in him, the invitations he sent out with his pretty brown eyes meant he got felt up every time he went to the bar, and he tended to always hang out at the bar. Jo got some incredible shots of Mitch running his hands over a sloe-eyed Sam onstage, but Randy's favorites were the candids of Kyl pressing a ready-to-whimper Sam against the wall. There were some fantastic shots of Emma and Steve cutting loose as well, and Randy had seen the two of them making lots of kinky new friends.

Randy himself had hands in his pants every time he hit the dance floor, and he had several prospects for post-reception shenanigans. But with hours left before the bar had to close, Sam caught Randy's hand and led him aside.

"What is it, Peaches?" Randy ducked into the stairwell with Sam, bending close to listen. "Is something wrong?"

"Nothing's wrong." Sam kissed him on the cheek. "Thank you for a wonderful wedding day. It was perfect."

"You're welcome. It was my pleasure." Randy smiled and stroked his cheek. "Let me know when you're ready, and I'll show you your honeymoon suite."

"I'm ready now."

That admission seared the edge of Randy's happiness, because he didn't want the night to end. He didn't let on, though, squeezing Sam's shoulder and glancing up toward the bar. "I'll tell Mark I'm taking off and will be back in a little bit. You go grab Mitch."

Sam caught his hand, not letting him leave. "You won't be back in a little bit. Not for a couple hours at least, I'm hoping."

Randy frowned at him. "What do you mean?"

The look on Sam's face was so tender it got Randy right in the gut. "You're coming with us. Into the honeymoon suite. I want you to play with us, Randy. Tonight. In fact, first I want to play with just you. Mitch wants that too."

Randy didn't know what to say. Surely he couldn't have heard right. *Play. Just you.* He shook his head, trying to clear it. "But this is your wedding night. You don't want to be with me *tonight*."

Sam took Randy's face in his hands and stared at him with a gaze a hell of a lot older than twenty-two had a right to be. "You're the reason we figured out how to be together. You're the reason we didn't get married at the courthouse and went home to fuck on the couch to christen the union. But even outside of that, you're part of us too, Randy. I married Mitch, but I love you too. We both do. We want you tonight. Especially tonight." He trailed a hand down Randy's neck. "Plus it's really kinky, asking you to do me on my wedding night with my husband's permission."

It was—but it was also so sweet Randy thought he might break. It touched him, moved him…shattered him, really. He didn't deserve this. Nobody did.

He kissed Sam on the forehead, because he couldn't kiss him on the mouth. Shutting his eyes, he drew a deep breath of his boy, thanking whatever divine power had led Sam into his life. Then he pinched Sam's ass.

"There's a pair of sweats in that bag Liam got your costume out of. Go put them on—but don't take off those shorts. That's gonna be my job, Peaches."

Sam smiled, kissed Randy on the cheek, and hurried up the stairs, his cute leather-clad ass bouncing all the way.

Randy watched it go. Then he went to find one of the guys, to let them know they needed to clean up and shut down, because he wasn't coming back before closing time.

CHAPTER NINE

THE HONEYMOON SUITE Randy had reserved was at a fancy downtown Des Moines hotel.

It wasn't far from the Saddle, but they'd all been drinking, and it had dipped below freezing, so they piled into a cab to get to their final destination. Sam sat between the two of them, snuggling Mitch, holding Randy's hand. Mitch stroked Sam's leg, body buzzing with alcohol, brain replaying all the fun he'd had at the party. He'd particularly enjoyed meeting Kyl and Mark, and it was clear that with some negotiation between boyfriends/husbands, there was some fun to be had there. Jo had often stepped outside to take a break from what she described as "too many people," so Mitch got to talk to her at the smokers' bench. Mary had always been everywhere, happy, loving, mothering. She wrote murder mysteries and promised to send one for Mitch to read. Jess had been fun too, especially once someone pulled out the karaoke machine. In fact, she and Sam had gotten into something of a duel.

Sam was quiet now, though Mitch knew he wasn't sleepy. There was a lot of night left to go.

Randy, though, seemed nervous.

Randy led them through the lobby of the fancy hotel, making wisecracks, but the smart remarks only highlighted his unsteadiness. As they rode the elevator, Mitch began to worry he'd made a mistake, having Sam issue this invitation. He couldn't work out why Randy felt so awkward at receiving it, but that was sure what it looked like was happening.

"Here we are." Randy stepped into the hall and gestured toward a door, flapping a plastic key. "Your temporary palace."

He gave them a tour—their suitcases had already appeared, as well as snacks and drinks and a basket of toys by the bed. They had two rooms, a living area with a wet bar, fireplace, and couches, and a bedroom with a large bath. On the bar were a bottle of champagne and two glasses, and a note from the hotel offering their congratulations.

"I had to enlist help in getting the room." Randy cracked the champagne and poured two glasses. "It was reserved, and I couldn't find anything else I liked. So Crabtree arranged for a glitch in the reservation system, and, voilà, the room was yours." He handed Sam and Mitch glasses of champagne. His smile was so thin it wobbled. "Cheers to you."

Mitch was about to say something when Sam put his glass down, crossed to the wet bar, and picked up a glass from beside the sink. After pouring champagne into it, he passed the fancy glass back to Randy and lifted the other in salute. "Cheers to us."

Mitch raised his drink as well. "To *us*."

Randy didn't raise his glass. In fact, he couldn't look them in the eye. "So…I was thinking. It was nice of you to offer…that, Sam, but this is your night. I don't belong here right now."

"What are you talking about?" Sam set his glass on the counter. "Randy, of course you do."

"No, I don't." Randy bit the words off, and when he set his glass beside Sam's, his hand shook. "This is *your* wedding night. Not mine."

Mitch put his drink down as well. "You're part of this, Skeet. You know that."

He'd never seen Randy this undone. "I'm not. I just helped set it up."

You want to be a part of this. You want your own version of this. Not with us, either. Your own. Mitch put a hand on Randy's shoulder, ran it down his back. "You're part of us. Someday we'll be sending you off at your wedding—"

Randy snorted.

Mitch pressed on. "—but right now whatever this is, it's ours, and we say you're part of us. Jesus, Skeet, you've seen how much we fuck up without you."

Randy averted his gaze, staring hard at the wall above the bar. "I'm not moving to Iowa, and you're not moving to Vegas. Same shit, different year."

"We're coming to visit. A lot." Sam slid his arms around Randy's waist and kissed his neck. "Every time I get a break, we're heading to see you. And you can come here anytime."

Randy didn't embrace Sam back. "If it's not cold here, it's humid. Sometimes it's both. And you can't come visit. If you're not in school, you're working."

"I'll take time off. I have the feeling my aunt will be a little more understanding with me now. Which was you, wasn't it? You talked to her. You fixed her, like you fix everything." Sam kissed Randy's jaw, the space below his ear. "Let us fix you."

Now Randy stared at the ceiling, his expression naked and sad. "I don't want to be your fucking also-ran."

"You're not an also-ran. You're Randy." Mitch closed the distance between them and slid his hand between Sam's mouth and Randy's cheek, turning his friend's face to his own. "You're ours. Quit trying to push yourself out and let us pull you in."

Randy shut his eyes tight. "Cactus."

Mitch held his chin, hard, and kissed him on the mouth. "You can't use your safe word when it isn't a game."

With a heavy sigh, Randy slumped, resting his head on Mitch's forehead. Mitch touched his face, ran fingers over his friend's jaw as Sam kissed his way down his neck and chest, unzipping his leather coat to reveal the bare skin beneath. When Sam went to his knees and unworked the lacings of Randy's leather pants, Mitch moved to stand behind, kissing Randy's neck, threading his hand into Sam's hair. As Sam took Randy's cock into his mouth, Mitch pulled the leather jacket away and massaged Randy's chest, arms, shoulders. Never did he stop kissing him.

Somewhere in the middle of the blowjob Randy came back to life—his hand threaded deeper into Sam's hair, he pushed against Mitch, and thrust into Sam's mouth. He turned his head toward Mitch, reaching to grip the back of Mitch's head.

"This is your night," he whispered, one last attempt to get away.

Mitch slid his tongue into Randy's ear. "That means we get to spend it however we want."

In the end it was both what Mitch had suggested and it wasn't. It was Randy and Sam who hit the bed first, Sam gasping and pleading and flying away as Randy ruthlessly stripped him and bent him in half to suck Sam's sweaty balls into his mouth—but they weren't alone, because Mitch stood in the doorway. As Randy tortured Sam, he called out to Mitch, asking if he liked watching somebody else fuck his husband. He asked it over and over.

"Sure," Mitch replied, every time. "Especially when it's you."

Randy took Sam from behind, both of them kneeling on the bed as they faced Mitch. Randy pulled Sam's head back by his hair as he thrust inside. "Look at your husband. Show him how much you love this. *Show him.*"

Sam did. And it was glorious.

This was a fucking wedding night.

After they were spent the first time, Mitch joined them on the bed, pressing Sam between them, stroking them both, kissing Sam. When he recovered, Randy began kissing Sam too, up the back of his neck, around his ear, down his cheek, carefully staying away from their joined mouths.

It just sort of happened. Sam turned, stopped, and then Mitch nudged him the rest of the way—it was brief, but for a fraction of a second, the three of them kissed. Then they kissed again, all three at once—it was a little impossible, but it was perfect in a way Mitch didn't know how to describe. It was breaking his rule, and it made him nervous, but it felt right.

He told himself, when it came to Randy, he needed to think about breaking that rule in the future.

They fucked a thousand ways that night, and they went through every toy in the basket. After watching a delicious session between a wicked Randy, a whimpering Sam, and a very fat plug, Mitch suggested they give Sam what he'd been begging for. With Mitch on the bottom, Sam in the middle, Randy behind, they double-penetrated him for the second time. Mitch watched Sam's face the whole time, a picture of pain and ecstasy—and always, there was Randy, lost in much of the same. Mitch pushed Sam back, wanting a full-frontal view, and he ran his hand down Sam's chest. Mitch's fingers tangled in the hair of Sam's groin as Randy wrapped his arms around Sam's shoulders, whispered into his neck, and thrust, sending tears streaming out of Sam's eyes.

Then Randy pulled out, pushing Sam forward. "Finish." He jacked himself, aiming his cock over Sam's back. "I want to watch the pair of you. And then I'm going to come all the fuck over you both."

That was how it ended. Mitch anchored his feet and pumped up hard and fast, until Sam's eyes rolled back into his head and he came in a sharp rush, and that was when Mitch let go. Sam collapsed against him, gasping and shaking, while behind them Randy jerked himself until he sprayed them with his cum.

They spooned together on the bed after, Sam falling immediately to sleep, Mitch drifting in and out until he woke realizing it was only he and Sam tangled in the sheets. Extricating himself carefully so as to not wake his husband, Mitch stepped into a pair of boxers and padded out into the front room.

Randy stood at the bar, drinking champagne from the water glass. When he saw Mitch, he lifted it in a toast. "Seemed a shame to waste booze."

Mitch picked up one of the other glasses, clicked Randy's in toast, and took a drink. It wasn't bad, as champagne went. He swished the amber liquid around before sipping it. "So. This is somewhere I never thought I'd end up, when I picked you up in that parking lot all those years ago when we first met."

"Tell me about it." Randy's tone was wry, but he was relaxed now. Still a little sad, but not so jagged as he'd been when they first arrived. He arched an eyebrow at Mitch. "Was this your way of telling me if Iowa allowed plural marriages, you two would adopt me?"

Mitch considered his words. "Not exactly. I still think you need one of your own. A husband, I mean."

Randy snorted. "*That* is beyond the realm of possibility, Old Man."

"That's the thing about life. It's a crazy-assed road, and there's no map. You never know what lies ahead." He leaned on the counter and looked Randy dead in the eye. "What I'm telling you is that until you find your somebody, or even if you never do, you have us. Like this. You want to move in, travel with us, it's done. You want to be off on your own, then come back and hang with us, it's fine. You want to marry somebody and be exclusive and we're just friends, no problem. But you're still part of us, always. We're yours, and you're ours. And if you try and shove us off on our own again like that, leaving yourself out in the cold because you think we don't want you, I'll kick your ass."

Randy rolled his eyes, but the gesture didn't quite take, and eventually he sighed and lifted his glass again. "Here's to hooch and cake. I think it's safe to say we did it better than we had a right to."

Mitch lifted his glass too, clinking against the side of Randy's with a wry smile. "Always, Skeet. Always."

Dying to know who could possibly lead Randy Jansen into his happily ever after? Not ready to let go of your Special Delivery boys just yet? Continue the adventure in *Double Blind*, available now wherever books are sold.

Know when to show your hand…and when to hedge your bets.

Randy Jansen can't stand to just sit by and watch as a mysterious man throws money away on the roulette wheel, especially since Randy's got his own bet going as to the reason this guy is making every play like it's his last day on earth. The man's dark desperation hits Randy right in the gut. Half of him warns that getting involved is a sucker's bet, and the other half scrambles for a reason—any reason—to save the man's soul.

Ethan Ellison has no idea what he's going to do with himself once his last dollar is gone—until Randy whirls into his life with a heart-stealing smile and a poker player's gaze that sees too much. Randy draws Ethan into a series of wagers that leads to a scorching kiss by midnight, but he isn't the only one with an interest in Ethan's vulnerability. Soon they're both taking risks that not only play fast and loose with the law, but with the biggest prize of all: their hearts.

ABOUT THE AUTHOR

Heidi Cullinan has always enjoyed a good love story, provided it has a happy ending. Proud to be from the first Midwestern state with full marriage equality, Heidi is a vocal advocate for LGBT rights. She writes positive-outcome romances for LGBT characters struggling against insurmountable odds because she believes there's no such thing as too much happy ever after. When Heidi isn't writing, she enjoys cooking, reading, playing with her cats, and watching anime, with or without her family. Find out more about Heidi at heidicullinan.com.

Did you enjoy this book?

If you did, please consider leaving a review online or recommending it to a friend. There's absolutely nothing that helps an author more than a reader's enthusiasm. Your word of mouth is greatly appreciated and helps me sell more books, which helps me write more books.

OTHER TITLES IN THIS SERIES

SPECIAL DELIVERY

Sam knows he'll never find the excitement he craves in Middleton, Iowa. Then Sam meets Mitch, an independent, long-haul trucker. When Mitch offers to take him on a road trip west, Sam jumps at the chance. One minute Mitch is the star of Sam's X-rated fantasies, the next he's a perfect gentleman. And when they hit the Las Vegas city limit, Sam finds out why: Randy. Sam grapples with the meaning of friendship, letting go, growing up—even the meaning of love—because no matter how far he travels, eventually all roads lead home.

DOUBLE BLIND

Randy can't stand to just sit by and watch as a mysterious man throws money away on roulette. The man's dark desperation has him scrambling for a reason—any reason—to save his soul. Ethan has no idea what he's going to do with himself once his last dollar is gone—until Randy whirls into his life with a heart-stealing smile and a poker player's gaze that sees too much. Soon they're both taking risks that not only play fast and loose with the law, but with the biggest prize of all: their hearts.

THE TWELVE DAYS OF RANDY

Randy and Ethan are ready to enjoy their first Christmas at home together, but when Crabtree ropes Randy into wily holiday antics, Ethan feels left out in the cold. When Herod's new owner discovers his husband only plays at being an imp to hide a Christmas spirit bigger and tackier than Las Vegas, Ethan vows to find a way to have his cake and eat it too. Especially if Randy's the one jumping out of the middle.

TOUGH LOVE

Chenco Ortiz harbors fierce dreams of being a drag star on a glittering stage, but when leatherman Steve Vance introduces him to the intoxicating world of sadomasochism, he finds strength in body and mind he's never dreamed to seek—strength enough maybe to save his tortured Papi too.

OTHER BOOKS BY HEIDI CULLINAN

There's a lot happening with my books right now! Sign up for my **release-announcement-only newsletter** on my website to be sure you don't miss a single release or rerelease.

www.heidicullinan.com/newssignup

Want the inside scoop on upcoming releases, automatic delivery of all my titles in your preferred format, with option for signed paperbacks shipped worldwide? Consider joining my Patreon.

www.patreon.com/heidicullinan

THE ROOSEVELT SERIES
Carry the Ocean (also available in French)
Shelter the Sea
Unleash the Earth (coming soon)
Shatter the Sky (coming soon)

LOVE LESSONS SERIES
Love Lessons (also available in German; French coming soon)
Frozen Heart
Fever Pitch (also available in German)

Lonely Hearts (also available in German)
Short Stay
Rebel Heart (coming soon)

THE DANCING SERIES
Dance With Me (also available in French; Italian coming soon)
Enjoy the Dance
Burn the Floor (coming soon)

MINNESOTA CHRISTMAS SERIES
Let It Snow
Sleigh Ride
Winter Wonderland
Santa Baby

CHRISTMAS TOWN SERIES
The Christmas Fling

THE SPECIAL DELIVERY SERIES
Special Delivery
Hooch and Cake
Double Blind
The Twelve Days of Randy
Tough Love

CLOCKWORK LOVE SERIES
Clockwork Heart
Clockwork Pirate (coming soon)
Clockwork Princess (coming soon)

TUCKER SPRINGS SERIES
Second Hand (written with Marie Sexton)
(available in French)
Dirty Laundry (available in French)
(more titles in this series by other authors)

SINGLE TITLES
Nowhere Ranch (available in Italian)
Family Man (written with Marie Sexton)
A Private Gentleman
The Devil Will Do
Hero
Miles and the Magic Flute

NONFICTION
Your A Game: Winning Promo for Genre Fiction (written with Damon Suede)

Many titles are also available in audio and more are in production. Check the listings wherever you purchase audiobooks to see which titles are available.

CPSIA information can be obtained
at www.ICGtesting.com
Printed in the USA
BVHW081911020119
536778BV00003B/344/P